Glutton for You

NATALIE FALKENWRATH

BENTON HOUSE PUBLISHING

Benton House Publishing

bentonhousepublishing.com

ISBN 978-1-952057-06-9 (Paperback)

ISBN 978-1-952057-07-6 (eBook)

For more information about the author and

upcoming books, please visit

nataliefalkenwrath.com

For the lady love of my life, you inspire me every day

Chapter 1: Mel

Mel Park was filled with hope and excitement when she arrived at the modern one-bedroom apartment she shared with her girlfriend, Heidi. She had big news—news she couldn't wait to share with the woman she loved. Mel hummed to herself as she pulled out her keys, but when she reached to unlock the door, she found that it was already unlocked.

"That's weird," she mumbled. Heidi was normally very cautious about keeping the door locked and talked often of her fear of unwanted visitors—namely, her ex-boyfriend. She'd been hiding from him for as long as Mel had known her. It was the reason why Mel's name was the only one on the lease to the apartment they shared, and why Heidi only ever used cash. It was Heidi's money that paid the rent and utilities, but it all went through Mel.

Mel didn't mind helping out—it was good to have something to offer; she'd been otherwise dependent on

Heidi since moving to the city six months prior. But she didn't need to be dependent anymore—not after today. Because today Mel had finally gotten a job.

Mel couldn't wait to tell Heidi all about North River Bar and Grill and her employers, Pat and Nancy. Pat and Nancy were a sweet older lesbian couple of the 'flannel and jeans, pack the dogs in the Suburu, we're going hiking' variety. And they were immediately Mel's idols.

The job itself was just a basic bartending gig, but her bosses had given Mel hope that it could one day lead to more. She was interested in working in the restaurant industry; she loved to be innovative with her own culinary creations. It was her personal twists on classic cocktails that had landed her the job. And it had been hinted that if things worked out, she might get the chance to expand her creative contributions to the kitchen. *Maybe I can cook something fun to celebrate tonight.*

Mel opened the door and stepped inside. Something immediately felt out of place, although Mel couldn't pinpoint what it was. The apartment looked the same as ever—if a bit empty.

Many times when Mel got home, she would find Heidi sitting in the living room on the yellow mid-century sofa, wrapped in her patchwork quilt, feet propped on the coffee table, watching TV on the apartment's large flatscreen. Heidi had a weak spot for trashy daytime television. Today, however, the screen was black and the sofa unoccupied.

Mel stepped past the living room into the kitchen. It was clean—aside from a few dishes stacked in the white farmhouse sink and discarded mail sitting scattered on the butcher-block countertop. Mel hung her jacket on one of the kitchen table's four wooden chairs.

"Heidi?" She called out as she walked further into the apartment, past the broom closet and bathroom. As she got closer, Mel could hear a faint thumping sound emanating from the bedroom. The door was closed. Mel reached for the knob. "Babe? I've got good news—"

Mel opened the door and froze, her words dying on her lips; her previous excitement crushed under the weight of what she found there. Her girlfriend—the woman she loved—in bed, furiously fucking a large, dark-haired man. She was riding him cowgirl style, slamming her body rhythmically onto his, her large breasts bouncing with the motion as she moaned softly in pleasure.

"Heidi?!" Mel gasped. "Heidi, what are you doing?!"

Heidi didn't stop; she arched her body and threw back her head—her long, blonde-streaked hair brushing the top of the man's hairy thighs as she continued to ride him.

When Heidi brought her head back up, she caught Mel's eye. She gave Mel a wide, dopey grin before turning her attention back to the man between her legs.

She's high. Mel could tell by her vacant, blissful expression. She looked at the man. He was unfamiliar to her, but by the way his eyes rolled back in his head, it wasn't hard to guess that he was high as well. Mel stood frozen; her whole body felt like it had gone numb. She didn't know what to do. Heidi and her male companion apparently had no intention of stopping for her sake.

"Yeah, baby, you're so hot," the man moaned encouragingly, his words slurred with intoxication.

"You like this, yeah?" Heidi slurred back.

Mel managed to regain control of her motor function and backed slowly out of the room. She didn't know what else to do, so she stumbled out to the living room and sat down on the couch. Her mind was in a fog of confusion and hurt.

Mel had thought Heidi was her soulmate. She was functionally the only person Mel had in her life. When her parents had kicked her out, Heidi had been there to catch her. She'd made Mel feel like she finally had a home and somebody who cared about her—somebody who accepted her for who she was. Her parents were too worried about her sins and her mortal soul to care about her as a person. They'd cut her out to 'save' her, and it had hurt, but Heidi's love and attention had soothed the pain of that.

Mel had moved halfway across the country for her; she'd left everybody she'd ever known for the chance to live as her authentic self with the person she loved. Heidi was her entire world, and now that world was imploding.

Mel ran shaking fingers through her hair. The smooth black strands slipped through her fingers. She brushed her hand down, across the short, buzzed hair below.

Mel had always considered herself a pretty tough person. She'd been through a lot growing up as a closet lesbian in a conservative Christian community. She'd rebelled in every way she could control as a teen—hair, tattoos, piercings—but when she'd finally come out, that was the last straw. Her parents could live with the shame of having a wild daughter, but having a gay one was too much.

Mel had never let her parents see her cry. She'd screamed back and slammed the door when she finally left that house for good. Mel hated crying, and as a rule she didn't. But now tears were spilling silently down her cheeks. The anger she should have felt—the anger that would have kept the tears at bay—was obfuscated by the deep pain of heartbreak and betrayal. Mel had learned at a young age that she couldn't trust her family, but she had trusted Heidi.

Mel waited in the living room for what seemed like an eternity. Eventually, her tears stopped but the shaking did not. She ran trembling fingers across one of the tattoos on her forearm. *There is no emotion, there is peace*, she told herself and willed it to be true. She touched the inked lettering under her arm. *Come what come may. 'Time and the hour runs through the roughest day.'*

Mel repeated these words to herself until her hands were no longer shaking and her heart rate had dropped. She still didn't have the energy for anger, but she felt some sense of control.

With a deep breath, Mel made her way back to the bedroom. Heidi and the man were both passed out cold. Heidi's face, which Mel had always found entrancingly beautiful, was almost unrecognizable to her now. The Heidi that lay there—red-faced and snoring—was like a stranger to her.

Mel went to Heidi's side and shook her. "Heidi. Heidi, wake up," she urged. Heidi muttered something unintelligible and rolled over. Mel shook her harder. "Heidi, you have to wake up. You have to tell me what's going on." Mel kept her voice sharp but quiet; she didn't want to wake the man.

He was tall and muscular with a nose that looked like it had been broken more than once. He had the appearance of a man who hit first and asked questions later. And Mel wanted to be the one asking the questions.

"Heidi, get up!" Mel demanded.

"Go away, Mel," Heidi murmured.

Hearing her own name—a confirmation that Heidi was aware enough to recognize her for who she was— made something inside of Mel snap.

"Fuck you, Heidi! Wake up! Wake up and talk to me, damnit!" Mel shouted, suddenly furious.

Heidi grunted and tried to roll away from her again. Mel picked up a glass of water from the nightstand and dumped it on Heidi's face. That did the trick. Heidi came to, sputtering and cursing.

"Bitch!" she spat, sitting up and wiping her face.

"I'm the bitch?! I came home to find you in bed with a *man*! You didn't even stop fucking when I got here! What the hell, Heidi? What's going on?" Mel could feel the effects of anger and adrenaline coursing through her blood. "Who is that?" She demanded, pointing to the man.

"My husband, Brad," Heidi said simply.

Mel blinked at her. "Your *what*?"

Heidi shrugged like it was no big deal. "My husband, okay? You caught me. I'm still married."

"Are you back together?" Mel asked, confused and incredulous.

"Yes."

"What about us?"

Again Heidi shrugged. She looked ready to fall back asleep.

"How high are you? What did you take?" Mel asked, looking her girlfriend over until she found the telltale marks on her arm. She grabbed Heidi's wrist.

"Heroin? Are you kidding me? You said you'd never do that again. You said—"

"I said a lot of things!" Heidi yanked her arm away from Mel's grasp. "And I don't need your judgment about any of it! In fact, I don't need you at all!"

"How long has this been going on?" Mel demanded.

Heidi narrowed her eyes. "Always. I was always going to end up with Brad. This was a fun little *project,* but it was never going to last." Her voice was filled with cold indifference.

"You've been stringing me along?" Mel asked, disbelieving. "To what end?" It didn't make any sense. What had they been doing these last six months, if not building a life together?

"I'm sorry it wasn't the little lesbian fairy tale you wanted but—"

"Get out," Mel growled. "Get out *now.*"

"Or what?"

"Or I call the cops." Mel glared at her, but Heidi seemed nonplused. "I'm serious, Heidi. Get out, or I call the police and the landlord. *My* name is on the lease. The landlord doesn't even know you. So if you don't want to be arrested…"

"You wouldn't." There was a hint of fear growing behind Heidi's big blue eyes.

Mel pulled out her phone and held it so that Heidi could clearly see the keypad. She typed in 9-1-1 and then let her finger hover over the call icon. "Try me," she dared. She didn't want to call the police, but she wasn't bluffing either. After a few seconds of silent glaring, Heidi seemed to get the message. She stood and began to dress. She shimmied into her jeans and pulled a tank top over her bare chest.

"Brad!" Heidi smacked the man, who was still sound asleep. "Brad! Get up!" She hit him again and he began to stir.

"What's going on?" he asked, rubbing his eyes.

"My bitch of an *ex*-girlfriend is kicking us out," Heidi explained as she sat down and pulled on her socks.

"What?"

Heidi zipped up her boots and stood, arms crossed. "She says she's gonna call the cops."

"Shit. Fine." Brad stumbled to his feet and Heidi helped him locate his clothes. While he dressed, Heidi threw a few things into the green canvas gym bag sitting at the foot of the bed.

Mel caught a glance at the contents of the bag, then wished she hadn't. She'd never seen heroin in person before but she knew drug paraphernalia when she saw it.

"Hurry it up," Mel said, uncomfortable with the knowledge that Heidi was using again. She'd never known Heidi when she was using; they'd met after Heidi had gotten clean. She'd sworn that that life was behind her, but apparently, it had just been on pause. Mel felt like she didn't even know her girlfriend anymore, if she ever had.

"You're being a real cunt, you know that?" Heidi grumbled. "I paid for this place. This is my shit. I'm coming back for it."

"And I'll let you. When you're alone and sober. But right now, if you do anything other than get the hell out, I will hit this button and you will go to jail. I'm sure the cops would be pretty interested in your duffle bag there."

Heidi clutched the bag closer to her body and glared. "You're going to regret this," she hissed.

"Regret what?" Mel spat back. "This was all you! You did this, Heidi. These are your actions; I'm just reacting to them. Now get out."

Mel followed the two out of the bedroom and watched them until they were out the door. When they were gone, she locked the door and slid the chain into place. *What the fuck just happened to my life?*

~ ~ ~

The next morning, Mel had no choice but to get up and go to work as if nothing had happened. It was the first day of her new job and Pat would be waiting for her—expecting the friendly, eager young woman who she'd hired only yesterday. Mel tried desperately to be that person. She dressed in clean black slacks and a white button-down shirt worn open over a white t-shirt. She brushed and braided the long part of her hair into a tight French braid. Her eyes were still rimmed with red from crying, but she hoped Pat wouldn't notice.

Mel arrived at North River two minutes early, walking in through the back employee entrance for the first time. She walked through the kitchen. It was bright and clean. Mel eyed the large gas range, flattop grill, and industrial ovens with excitement and maybe a little jealousy—wishing she had the qualifications to spend time cooking in such a lovely kitchen. She continued through to the bar, which overlooked the dining room.

North River wasn't fancy, but it was classic. The furnishings were older but in good repair. The lighting was dim but not dim enough to make Mel suspect it was kept that way to hide the stains—something that had been a well-known fact about the one bar in her hometown.

The bar itself, where Mel would be working most of the time, had a long, polished wood surface. Rows of stemmed glasses hung above, with pints and tumblers behind the bar. The shelves of liquor and long row of taps would be at her back when standing at the bar, looking out at the dining room. Cheaper booze, mixers, and garnishes would be in front of her, below the bar level, easily accessible.

During her interview, Mel had impressed Pat by finding most things intuitively as she made a few of her signature drinks. Being back there again today, Mel already felt at home.

Pat met Mel at the bar. She was jovial but efficient in the way that she walked Mel through all the ins and outs of what she would be doing. She gave her the breakdown of how and when she would be expected to do prep, and the procedure for closing down at the end of the night. North River's staffing was lean, so Mel would be expected to regularly do clopens—both closing late at night and opening early the next morning. That would make for some long days, but long days sounded *wonderful* to Mel, who was dreading just about everything in her life outside of that warm little restaurant.

Mel was introduced to Sebastian, who acted as both host and server during the day, and Carlos, the cook. Nancy, Pat's wife, also cooked and planned menus, but she wouldn't be in until later. Pat handled most of the staffing and was known to jump behind the bar from time to time.

"We don't get a ton of lunch traffic, but we do have our regulars," Pat explained as they set to open.

"Any characters I should look out for?" Mel asked, already busy prepping.

"Oh, yeah." Pat laughed. "You can't have a bar without a few characters. They're mostly harmless and I'm sure you'll get to know them quickly. Keep an eye out for Gene, though. He likes to give new staff a hard time and his humor can be a little… old-fashioned. Don't take anything he says seriously or personally, and you'll be fine."

Mel nodded. "Old-fashioned" was likely code for racist, sexist, or homophobic. As a gay, Asian woman, Mel was well experienced in dealing with all three and—for better or worse—had gotten quite good at not letting that kind of bullshit get to her.

"And Mark," Pat continued. "He won't give you trouble exactly, he's a really sweet guy, but he will drink himself unconscious if you let him."

"What if that happens?" Mel asked.

"We like to kick him out before he gets there, but I'm a sucker for sappy drunks and will put him in a cab. I've even let him sleep it off in one of the back booths once or twice."

Mel nodded. A bar's regulars were a part of its culture. Given that the owners were gay, Mel had to wonder if that had an effect on the clientele. "Do you get many queer customers?" she asked.

Pat shook her head. "Not a ton. We're not exactly flying a rainbow flag. 'Lesbian bars' don't tend to do too well, so we're just a bar run by lesbians. We have some friends and acquaintances from the community who come by regularly, but they're mostly dining room types. You know: date nights, family dinners out with kids—not many come here single and looking. It's just not that type of place." Pat gave Mel a sideways look. "I wouldn't expect you'll have women coming in here to hit on you. Sorry if that's a disappointment."

"No, not at all," Mel said quickly. "I was just asking out of curiosity. I have a girlfriend anyway." It didn't feel like a lie, even though Mel knew it probably was. The reality of her newly single status hadn't fully sunk in yet. And she was far from ready to start thinking about being 'hit on' by other women. If men tried to flirt with her, she knew how to politely brush them off. She gave off pretty strong lesbian vibes, but as butch as she tried to present herself, she's never been able to avoid male attention entirely. But that was just life, and not unique to bartending.

"Well, if you're all settled in here," Pat said. "I'll be in back. Let me know if you need anything. Good luck and welcome aboard!"

"Thanks. I'm really happy to be here," Mel replied, and she meant it.

~ ~ ~

Within a few days, Mel was moving around the bar as if she'd been there for years. She got a good rapport going with the regulars and was building a decent workplace friendship with Sebastian. He was young and gay and very easy to talk to. He'd been at North River for a couple of years and had all the best gossip.

The atmosphere was relaxed and Mel's slacks and button-down were soon replaced with the clothes she was most comfortable in: a t-shirt and jeans or cargo shorts. Pat and Nancy were always positive and friendly with her, even when correcting her work. And the tips were much better than Mel had expected from such a small hole-in-the-wall establishment. Overall, Mel was happy—when she was at North River.

Most days, Mel arrived home in the wee hours of the morning, showered, and passed out. Then she would wake up in the morning, dress, and go back to work. That was how she preferred it. She wanted to spend as little time as possible in the apartment she'd once shared with Heidi. But Pat wouldn't let her work until close every night. No matter how much Mel begged, Pat was insistent that she needed downtime in her life.

"You're a great employee, Mel," Pat had said. "I'm not going to let you burn yourself out in the first month. I want to keep you around for longer than that."

Mel had reluctantly given up and begrudgingly accepted her time off from work. But she still had no idea what to *do* with that time. She didn't want to spend any money. She still had the cash Heidi had given her—intended for paying rent—but she hated to use it.

Mel still hadn't heard from Heidi, and even if she had, she was determined to be self-sufficient now that she had her own real job. She canceled her cable and simplified her phone plan. The large TV sat useless in the living room. The only electronic entertainment at home was watching shows on her laptop with a Netflix account borrowed from a friend back home, and wi-fi stolen from a careless neighbor.

The one thing Mel spent money on was food. She cooked for herself with care. Every meal she made was an activity—the only activity she truly enjoyed doing alone in that memory-filled apartment.

~ ~ ~

"I think this might be my favorite sandwich here so far," Mel said to Sebastian, indicating the French Dip on her plate.

She was slowly eating her way through North River's menu. She wanted to be familiar with all of the food, not only to be able to advise customers, but also to inform her own dream of putting something of her own on that menu. She figured that trying everything would help her get a sense of what could fill a gap while fitting in with the general feel of the place. It was a fun endeavor and seemed to entertain Sebastian.

"Oh yeah? Why's that?" Sebastian asked. "Is it the, uh, general *look*?" He gestured at part of the sandwich and gave her a suggestive wiggle of his eyebrows.

"Are you asking if I like it because it looks like a vagina?" Mel asked with a laugh.

Sebastian shrugged. "I'm just saying. I know that's the sort of thing you're *into*." He shuddered dramatically and then dodged out of the way as Mel wound up to smack him in the arm.

"Oh, shut up," Mel said with a laugh. "I like it because it's good. The meat is tender and the 'au jus' is killer. I don't think I've ever had a French Dip with this much flavor without being too salty. I'm putting it in the 'winner' column for sure."

"So then what's in the 'loser' column?" Sebastian asked.

"Just you, buddy," Mel said with a wink. "Seriously though; I'm not dumb enough to make a 'loser' column. I do want to keep my job here, you know. Some things are just not quite as good as others."

"Such as what, the brats? I mean, they are *wieners*." Sebastian laughed at his own joke.

"No." Mel rolled her eyes

"What then?" Sebastian asked.

Mel ran her finger down the menu. "Well, the turkey club is kind of dry," she said.

"Maybe if you dunked that in the '*au jus*'," Sebastian suggested. He's said it as if he expected her to protest but Mel only laughed.

"Why not? Everything is better when dipped in something wet." She winked and Sebastian burst out laughing.

"You lesbians are too much," he snorted. "Hey, can you cover my tables while I take a long lunch?" Sebastian asked. "I have some errands to run; if I don't get to the bank today, I'm screwed."

"Yeah, no worries," Mel waved him off. "It's pretty quiet, and I don't mind the extra tips."

"Thanks, Mel. I owe you one."

When Sebastian had gone, Mel took out the photocopy she'd made of the menu and wrote a couple notes in the margins. She looked it over. She was making good progress. *I should try making some of these things at home*, she thought to herself. That sounded like a pretty good use of the excessive time off she had coming up. *It's not like I have anything else going on.*

Chapter 2: Amelia

"No, no, no," Amelia Fischer whispered under her breath. "Closed? How can it be closed? The Dragonfly is never closed on Monday." She reached out for the handle to the door but shrank back. Maybe somebody was inside doing work or cleaning—anything that didn't need to be interrupted by a silly girl rattling the door like she couldn't read a simple sign.

Amelia took a step back and sighed. There was nothing to be done about it—if the Dragonfly was closed, it was closed. She looked up at the gray skies that threatened rain. She didn't want to turn around and walk home; she wasn't very productive at home. Besides which, she wasn't sure she'd make it before the rain started. *I could try and get to the library*, she thought. The library was even further away than home, and in the opposite direction, but it was her second favorite place to work after the Dragonfly. *If I hurry maybe I could beat the rain.*

A fat raindrop hit the top of Amelia's head. *Or not.* Amelia looked desperately around the small square, wondering what she should do. The "up-and-coming" neighborhood she had moved to a year ago with her roommate Eliza was still struggling to "up and come." The tiny business district boasted a whole eight businesses, one up from when they'd first moved in. There was the Dragonfly on the northwest corner, next to which was a small real estate office that never seemed to be open. Amelia ducked under the office's striped awning as she considered her options.

Across the street to the east stood Felicity's—a kitschy little 'antique' store that sold unwanted items locals had inherited from deceased grandparents and forgotten great aunts twice removed. *I could kill a little time in there and hope the rain is brief.* As if in answer to her thought, thunder rumbled ominously. *Or not.*

To the south was the Venus Nail Salon attached to the world's smallest 'Chinese' restaurant, Dragon Wok. Amelia liked Dragon Wok—even though the smell of polish bled through from the nail salon. The food was decent and the people there were always friendly.

Unfortunately, they weren't open on Mondays. Not that the pungent little restaurant would have made an ideal workspace, but it might have been okay for a few hours. She could sip tea and eat spring rolls while she wrote. *Maybe if the Dragonfly is still closed tomorrow.* Amelia's tummy rumbled along with the thunder. She'd been planning on having a late breakfast of oatmeal and fruit while she worked. Now she was regretting not eating at home.

She rubbed her stomach and let her gaze move east, past the Dragon Wok. The block kitty-corner from Amelia's beloved Dragonfly was what her roommate half-jokingly referred to as the 'bad part of town.' The storefronts there were older and noticeably dingier. Amelia had only ever been inside one of the three open businesses on the southeast block: Middlegrove Market—a small, cluttered convenience store. The food there was overpriced but it was the closest thing to a grocery store in the area. Next door to that was a laundromat that made Amelia grateful for her in-unit washer and dryer.

The last business, which Amelia could barely see from her spot under the real estate office awning, was the North River Bar and Grill—or Blood River Mob-front as her roommate Eliza called it. Neither Amelia nor her roommate had ever entered the bar; they'd not so much as peeked inside. From a distance, all you could see through the long, dark windows was the faint light of the 'open' sign that seemed to always be on. It was on now. *Is it really open?* It never looked open, despite the sign. Amelia couldn't recall ever even seeing anybody come or go through the oddly small red front door.

With another crack of lightning, the sky opened up and the rain came down in sheets. The awning provided insufficient protection from the deluge and Amelia knew she needed to move. She tightened the straps on her backpack, checked for traffic, and then bolted across the intersection. Her initial plan had been to go to the convenience store for an umbrella or some other sort of protection but found herself skipping over puddles past the store to the red door of the restaurant.

In all the time she'd spent near but never inside North River, Amelia's imagination had worked out its own picture of what the bar would be like: dark and grungy, with old torn faux-leather booths, tobacco-stained walls, and the stench of warm beer—a shady hideout for bikers and drunkards.

As Amelia's eyes adjusted to the dim lighting, she was pleasantly surprised to find that North River was clean and homey. It had a sort of log cabin smokehouse feel to it, with its rough wooden furnishings and North Woods decor.

It looks so much bigger on the inside, Amelia mused. She wasn't the only one there—a handful of patrons were split between two dining tables and a lone older man sat at the bar—yet the place felt empty. The sign by the entrance said 'seat yourself' so Amelia found a booth in the corner and settled in, pulling her laptop and notebook from her backpack. She didn't know how long it would take for a server to show up at her table, so she dug into her work right away.

A few minutes later a voice from over Amelia's shoulder made her look up. "How are you doing today?" The owner of the voice smiled down at her and Amelia felt her heart leap into her throat. The server who stood at her table was one of the most attractive human beings Amelia had ever seen in her life. High cheeks, a delicate nose pierced with a silver ring, square chin, dark eyes, and smooth complexion. Her strong jaw and soft features gave her a sort of androgynous beauty. Her shiny black hair was long on top but shaved underneath.

Her ears were pierced several times each, and black and gray tattoos decorated her visibly strong arms and peeked up out of the neck of her t-shirt. She was like a soft butch beauty queen—someone directly out of Amelia's dreams.

"Can I start you with something to drink?" The mesmerizing server raised an eyebrow and Amelia snapped back into herself.

"Oh, hello!" Amelia responded suddenly as she shut her laptop with a bang. The woman laughed.

"Working on state secrets there?" she asked with a wry smile.

"What? No, I'm just…" Amelia stuttered, at a loss for how to respond to what was clearly just a good-natured joke. *Why do I never have snappy comebacks?* Her mind was blank, although she knew she'd think of something clever if given an hour or two. She kicked herself internally for being so slow. "I'll have a Diet Coke."

"One Diet Coke coming up. The menus are there on the table," the server said pointing to where the menus were tucked between the wall and condiment holder. "My name is Mel; please let me know if there's anything else I can get for you. I'll be right back with your drink."

"Thanks," Amelia said in a squeak. She could feel her cheeks burning. Mel turned and walked off toward the bar. Amelia watched her go. She was wearing a plain white t-shirt and sandy-brown cargo shorts with a black server's apron tied around her waist. The curve of her hips was subtle, and Amelia wondered what it would feel like to rest her hands on those boyish hips. Something about how Mel's white cotton t-shirt hung on her made Amelia desperate to touch her. It had been a very long time since Amelia had her hands on another woman, and she couldn't remember the last time someone had caught her eye so quickly. *What is it about this woman that's so… alluring?*

Amelia couldn't quite pin it down but from the instant she laid eyes on Mel, she was thoroughly entranced. Amelia opened her laptop again and tried to focus on her work, but she kept glancing over her shoulder—hoping to catch a glimpse of Mel on her way back with the soda. When several minutes passed with no sign of her, Amelia shut her laptop and opened a menu. She was hungry, but she didn't have a large budget for eating out and even if she had, heavy bar food would hardly have been her first choice. Amelia rubbed at her less-flat-than-ideal stomach. *The Diet Coke will make me feel less hungry. I should actually get some work done so that I'm not wasting money being here at all.* Amelia closed the menu and opened her laptop again.

"Sorry about the wait." Mel put the soda down next to Amelia, causing her to jump and slam her laptop shut for the second time.

"Don't worry, I don't make a habit of reading over my customer's shoulders," Mel assured her, and Amelia felt her cheeks warm again.

"No, it's not… it's okay, it's just a stupid article I'm writing—or trying to write," Amelia said.

"Are you a writer?" Mel asked.

"Uh, sort of?" Amelia ducked her head. No matter how many times she had this conversation, it never failed to make her flustered and embarrassed. And the addition of a super-hot girl wouldn't make it any easier. "I'm not writing anything real really. Just stuff to pay the bills."

"What non-real writing pays the bills? If you don't mind me asking." Mel looked into Amelia's face; her dark eyes seemed filled with genuine curiosity.

"Silly articles for… online. And uh, papers," Amelia mumbled.

"Papers?" Mel repeated. "Like newspapers?"

"No. Like school papers. I help college kids with their essays and whatnot," Amelia explained.

"Is that allowed? Like, isn't that kind of like helping them cheat?" Mel wrinkled her perfect little nose and Amelia felt her blush deepen.

"Yeah, it kind of is cheating. But the money is good…" Amelia ducked her head.

"Hey, no judgment, lady." Mel put a hand on Amelia's shoulder and Amelia lifted her eyes back to Mel's unfathomably attractive face. "We all gotta make a buck," she said with a wink that made Amelia feel as if she might melt right into the seat.

God, she's hot. How is she so hot? Mel had this calm confidence about her, this effortless cool that made her irresistibly sexy.

"Do you like the work?" Mel asked.

"It's a living," Amelia replied with a shrug.

"Speaking of 'a living', I should get back to mine. Unless you're ready to order?" Mel asked.

"Oh, uh…" Amelia fumbled to open the menu again, but she couldn't focus while Mel was watching her. "What's good here?" she asked.

"The French dip is my new favorite," Mel said, pointing. "Get it with fries. It's bomb."

"Okay, yeah, I'll have that," Amelia agreed without thinking.

"Great!" Mel flashed her a wide grin. Her teeth were all perfectly square and straight except one chipped tooth on the right that somehow made her smile even more charming. Amelia grinned back at her like a silly schoolgirl.

After Mel had walked off, Amelia came to her senses. "Why did I order that?" she whispered to herself. She looked at the description on the menu; she'd never had a French Dip before and wasn't even sure what it was. *Beef, cheese… what's au jus? And did I agree to fries?* Amelia's stomach churned anxiously at the thought of all that heavy food. *I had to order something, but I don't have to eat it,* she told herself, *think of it as rent on the table so I can write.*

She opened up her laptop once more and was finally able to get a decent draft of her article written before the food arrived.

"Getting your work done alright?" Mel asked as she put the giant steaming plate of food in front of Amelia.

"Oh, yeah, yes," Amelia replied, eyeing the sandwich with trepidation. "It's going well."

"Glad to hear it," Mel said. "Here's that French dip. Let me know if there's anything else I can get for you."

Maybe your phone number? Amelia thought. But she would never have the guts to say something like that. "I will," she said simply. Mel gave her another chest-warming smile before turning away and sauntering back off across the restaurant.

Amelia took a long, suspicious look at the sandwich in front of her before picking it up and taking one cautious bite. It wasn't terrible but it certainly wasn't worth the stomachache it was bound to give her. She set it back down again and resumed her work—switching gears to focus on the pile of college essays she had to 'revise.'

The job had been painful at first—doing schoolwork so that spoiled rich kids could get grades they didn't deserve and degrees they didn't earn—but Amelia was used to it now. She was able to separate the questionable ethics and enjoy being paid to write school papers—something she honestly enjoyed. It still wasn't what she really wanted to be doing; what she wanted was to write a book of her own. But she couldn't justify taking the time to indulge her fantasy of being a novelist when she could be earning money. It just didn't make sense. Not yet. Maybe in a few years, when she had some money saved up, perhaps then she could take time off to pour her heart into something she cared about.

Time slipped by quickly as Amelia worked, typing on her laptop, her mind fully engaged with the essay she was writing for some kid named Paxton. The topic was somewhat interesting: American Imperialism and the history of westward expansion. Paxton had given her plenty of material to work with and the prose came easily to Amelia.

"Didn't like your food?" Mel's voice made Amelia jump. She looked at her plate and the sandwich with one single bite taken out of it.

"Oh, no, it's fine, I just got distracted—"

"Did you try dipping it? It's no good unless you dip it," Mel advised pointing to the small bowl of greasy broth.

"Oh, no, I… okay." Amelia picked up the sandwich, dipped it, and with a nod of encouragement from Mel, brought the cold, soggy mess up to her mouth. Amelia was thoroughly expecting to hate it. To her surprise, the sandwich did taste better. Much better. Amelia bobbed her head in approval as she chewed.

"See? I told you," Mel said, crossing her tattooed arms across her small chest in a self-satisfied pose.

"It is, much better. Thank you." Amelia wished she hadn't waited until it was cold to give it a proper try. As if reading her mind, Mel scooped up the plate.

"Let me warm that up for you. I know you've been working; you deserve a warm lunch—now that you know what you were missing." Mel's eyes seemed to twinkle as she took the food away before Amelia had the chance to protest. When she returned with the warm sandwich, she set it down and then slid into the booth seat across from Amelia.

"There you go, lady," Mel said, pushing the food toward Amelia. "I'm about to go on break, but I'd love to hear more about this cheating for cash business you've got going. It sounds right out of Happy Days or something."

"Happy Days?" Amelia blinked, confused.

"Don't tell me you don't know the Fonz." Mel sat back, throwing one arm casually over the back of the booth.

Amelia shook her head. "No, I do, I just… I didn't get the connection," she said.

"Paying somebody to write papers for you. It just seems like a wacky scheme from an old sitcom—something the Fonz would cook up in his 'office.'" Mel ran one hand over the shaved part of the back of her head. Amelia tried not to be distracted by thoughts of running her fingers across Mel's short hair.

"Oh, well, I…" Amelia twisted a finger through her own boring brown ponytail. "I don't exactly write the essays for them, I just… I help flesh out their… ideas. They give me the information or outline—"

"And money. And then you write the paper for them," Mel finished with a lop-sided grin.

Amelia laughed and shook her head, letting her ponytail swing about her face. "Yeah, okay, you're right. It is kind of a scheme. The crazy thing is how often the ones paying me are actually the parents of the students for whom I'm writing."

"For whom? You are a smart one, aren't you? I bet they get good grades." Mel tilted her head. "If they don't get caught, that is," she amended thoughtfully. "What does happen if the students get caught?" Mel leaned forward, her eyes on Amelia's.

"They sign an agreement to take that risk. So that it never comes back to me." Amelia shrugged casually but inside her heart was hammering; her whole body felt warm under Mel's intense gaze. *Is she flirting with me?*

"Crazy." Mel flashed her another half-grin. "How'd you end up doing this, if you don't mind me asking?"

"A friend of a friend sort of thing," Amelia replied. "My roommate kind of hooked me up."

"Good roommate."

"Yeah."

There was a moment of silence where the two just looked at one another. Mel was a vision; Amelia felt drawn to her like a bee to a flower—a pull that made Amelia's chest tight and her breathing shallow. *Say something. Ask her out. Ask for her number.* Amelia opened her mouth, but she couldn't make the words come out.

Mel glanced at her watch. "Aw, shit." She stood up. "I've got to get back to the bar. Unless you want to…"

Amelia's heart jumped. *Is she going to ask me out?* "Unless I want to…?" Amelia looked intently into Mel's perfect face.

"Settle your tab now; otherwise I'll have to have my coworker close you out," Mel explained.

"Oh! Yeah, no, yeah, I'll close that now, that's fine," Amelia stumbled, hopping Mel couldn't tell that she was once again blushing. *She wasn't flirting; she's just being friendly because she's my server. Stop being silly*, Amelia admonished herself as she dug through her backpack for her wallet. She handed Mel her credit card. "You can just go ahead and run it."

Mel flipped the card over in her hand. "I'll do that. Thank you, Amelia," she said.

Amelia knew Mel was just reading her name off the card, but at the same time, her chest fluttered at the sound of her name on Mel's lips. "Yeah," was all she could manage before Mel walked off.

Amelia rolled her eyes at her own awkwardness. She knew she had a way with words on paper but listening to herself try to talk in real life was painful. Too flustered to get back to writing, Amelia continued to pick at her food until Mel returned with the credit card slip for her to sign.

"Have a good day, Amelia," Mel said. "I hope you come back again soon."

"You will," Amelia replied and then winced. "I mean, you too. And I will."

"Great!" Mel turned away once again, and once again Amelia was filled with a mixture of embarrassment and desire, as she watched Mel go.

Should I ever come back, knowing I'll just spend too much money, embarrass myself... Her stomach gurgled. *And make myself sick?* She knew she probably shouldn't. But at the same time, she knew she totally would. She was even looking forward to it.

~ ~ ~

When Amelia returned home, she immediately sought out her roommate and best friend, Eliza Cartwright. She found Eliza in the kitchen, still dressed for work in grey pants and a crisp blue button-up shirt, her blonde curls pulled up into a ponytail. *She must have only recently gotten home herself.*

"Hey, Eliza, guess what?" Amelia began to tell Eliza all about her day and most importantly about Mel. But Eliza wasn't one to just listen to a story, commentary-free—she had way too many opinions for that. Amelia was barely two sentences in when Eliza put her hands up for her to stop.

"Stop, slow down, rewind," Eliza said. "Are you seriously telling me you actually went inside Blood

River Mob-front? On purpose?" Eliza screwed up her face in horror.

"I didn't have anywhere else to go; the Dragonfly was closed—"

"And you were so distraught you decided to take your own life? Suicide by mobster?" Eliza asked. She gave Amelia a disapproving look. "You could have just come home, you know."

"It was raining, remember?"

"Whatever. So you survived, I take it?" Eliza pursed her lips and looked Amelia over. "You don't look so good." She sniffed the air. "And you smell like grease. So, what, it's not a mob-front death-trap, just a dive-bar grease-trap?"

"It's just a normal restaurant," Amelia protested. Although she did feel a little sick. She'd eaten far too much of that French dip and the pile of fries that it had come with. *Do I really smell bad too?* She sniffed at her shirt collar and Eliza tittered.

"Trust me, you smell. Now, what were you saying about the waitress?" Eliza turned away from Amelia to dig through the refrigerator.

"Mel. She's so hot." Amelia sighed. "We talked for a while. I'm thinking of going back tomorrow—"

"Oh no, are you developing a crush?" Eliza whipped back around. She put a hand on her hip and gave Amelia an exasperated look. "You're the worst when you have a crush, you know."

"I am not," Amelia protested.

Eliza scoffed. "Are you going to do that sad thing where you silently stalk her like you did with that construction chick?"

Amelia frowned deeply at her roommate. "I didn't stalk her," she grumbled.

"You walked by that building site every day. Twice a day! For a month!" Eliza rolled her eyes. "And you kept walking by in your little dresses and skirts… even the dudes started to notice you."

"They didn't notice me," Amelia said under her breath.

"Yeah, they did. *She* didn't. But they did." Eliza laughed. She reached into the refrigerator and pulled out a bottle of white wine. She silently lifted a glass to Amelia in question.

Amelia shook her head. "Can you just forget about the construction girl?"

Eliza poured herself a generous glassful. "How could I ever forget? You in your little sundress, getting all lubed up over some chick in Carhartt's—oh my God, didn't you actually go buy some of those God-awful tan overalls yourself? Like if you dressed like the construction chick then maybe she'd want to 'nail' you?"

"Why are we talking about this?" Amelia felt her face burn. She hated when Eliza teased her. But it was her roommate's favorite sport.

Eliza leaned against the counter, wine in hand. She batted her eyes at Amelia. "You started it, Amelia Bedelia. You were telling me about your new crush, remember? The chick from Grease River." Eliza gave Amelia an expectant look, as if this opening would in any way encourage her to be forthcoming about her 'new crush.'

Amelia looked at the ceiling. "It's no big deal. I just thought the server was cute."

"And you plan to go back."

"It's not like I'm going to stalk her," Amelia said. "I just... it's a good place to work when the Dragonfly isn't open. It's good to know I have a back-up option around here."

"A back-up with eye-candy," Eliza added.

"Sure. Yeah." Amelia felt her stomach turn. The food really wasn't sitting well in her stomach. Her body wasn't used to that much fatty food all at once. Amelia crossed her arms across her middle.

"Well, tell me what she looks like," Eliza pressed; if she noticed that Amelia wasn't feeling well she didn't show it. "She's dyke-y, I assume."

"Why do you assume that?" Amelia asked.

"Hello," Eliza sang. "You have a *type*."

"I do not," Amelia protested.

"Yeah, okay." Eliza snorted. "Maybe not. Maybe you've just been turned down by one too many fem girls and you're over-compensating… But she was butch, wasn't she?"

Amelia's stomach turned again. "Excuse me." She walked past Eliza and shut herself in the bathroom. She really didn't feel well.

"Come on, just tell me what she looks like," Eliza called through the bathroom door.

"Okay, fine. She's sort of tomboyish. Happy?" Amelia called back through gritted teeth as her body rebelled against the food she had consumed.

"Knew it. Thank you," Eliza said, sounding satisfied. "Now don't stink up the house; I have Becky coming over later and I don't need shit-stank fucking with my date."

Like anything I could do would derail your 'date,' Amelia thought. The nights when Becky came over were hardly 'dates.' They were more like booty-calls. And if Amelia thought a little intestinal distress would save her from having to listen to Eliza and Becky going at it all night long, she would have started eating Big Macs every time Becky was planning on coming around ages ago. Even explosive diarrhea was preferable to being in the vicinity of Eliza and Becky together.

When Amelia emerged from the bathroom, Eliza was busy lighting candles in the living room. She'd changed into a skin-tight tank top and tiny shorts that showed off a good portion of her petite round ass. Eliza was adorable and she knew it. She flaunted her perfect little body at the slightest provocation. For all the teasing Amelia endured about her 'little dresses and skirts,' she never wore anything half as revealing as Eliza did when she was in the mood for sex.

"You and Becky aren't going out then, I take it?" said Amelia.

"Nope," Eliza replied, shaking out her blonde hair and readjusting her bra. "It's just a casual night in. You know, pizza, TV, wine, and fucking."

"Splendid," Amelia muttered under her breath.

"Tell me more about your dive-bar tomboy." Eliza turned to Amelia. "Did you talk to her?"

Amelia shrugged. "A little. She asked about my work."

"Did you return the favor? Ask her about the exciting world of waitressing at a mob-front dive-bar?"

"It's not a mob-front." Amelia chewed her lip. Eliza's question made her realize that she'd answered all of Mel's questions but never asked Mel a thing about herself. "I didn't really... she kind of led the conversation. She seemed so interested in hearing about me... the way she looked at me... She was probably just being friendly. I really should have asked about her too..." Amelia sighed. She felt like an idiot.

Eliza gave Amelia an appraising look. "You really like her," she observed.

"Yeah, I do." Amelia nodded reluctantly. She hadn't felt this level of instant attraction for a while, and Mel had been so friendly. Amelia didn't want to let the opportunity slip by entirely. "I was thinking of going back. Maybe if I saw her again, I could tell if she liked me… What do you think?" Amelia asked.

"Tell me where is fancy bred, or in the heart or in the head?" Eliza replied cryptically in a sing-song voice.

"What now?" Amelia asked.

"How begot, now nourish'ed?" Eliza continued, and Amelia realized Eliza was reciting Shakespeare at her. Again. They'd both been English majors in college, it was how they'd met. But Eliza and Amelia had each taken very different paths within that major and after. Where Amelia loved writing and dreamed of being an author, Eliza had been all about consuming and analyzing literature. After college, Eliza had put her sharp, well-read mind to use in the field of law. That, and in annoying her roommate with literary references.

"What's your point?" Amelia asked.

"Reply, reply?" Eliza said, raising her eyebrows and giving Amelia an expectant look. "It's Merchant of Venice," Eliza hinted.

"I know," Amelia lied. "I'm just not getting your point."

"It is engendered in the eyes," Eliza continued. "With gazing fed and fancy dies. Let us all ring fancy's knell. I'll begin it, ding dong bell."

"Yeah, yeah, but what's your point?" Amelia crossed her arms and stared hard at Eliza.

"My point, ding-dong," Eliza said, "is not to get all worked up about this girl just because you fancy her look. You need to talk to her and get to know her, lest you get your heart set on somebody totally incompatible and waste your time pining over a relationship that would never work. The fact that you *look* but don't *do* is the death knell of your love-life."

"I'm not sure that was the point of that passage," Amelia replied warily.

Eliza waved a hand dismissively. "Whatever. My point is: this time, maybe engage more than your eyes and you might have a chance at finally getting that love story you so desperately want to write for yourself."

Eliza had a point, but Amelia wasn't about to concede anything. Eliza might be her roommate and best friend, but she could also be insufferably confident in her unasked-for opinions. *Why did I tell her about Mel in the first place again?*

The doorbell rang and Eliza's face lit up. She grinned. "At the very least, if you do something maybe you'll actually get laid." Eliza bounded over to the door.

"And speaking of getting laid…" she said as she opened the door for Becky.

"What's going on, sexy?" Becky said by way of greeting as she brushed into the room and wrapped Eliza in her arms.

"I was just telling Amelia how she needs to get laid," Eliza said with a little laugh. Amelia felt her face burn but Becky didn't spare her a glance.

"She's not the only one," Becky said, bending to kiss Eliza deeply. Becky was tall and thin, with long mousey hair and severe bangs. Amelia had never understood what Eliza saw in her. Becky wasn't bad looking exactly, she just wasn't particularly attractive either. And she always wore an expression of somebody smelling something unpleasant. Eliza should have been out of her league, at least in Amelia's opinion. But there she was, fiercely kissing Becky back and grabbing at her t-shirt like a horny teenager.

"I'll be in my room," Amelia said as she turned to go.

"You could join us," Becky said, pulling out of the kiss to look at Amelia over Eliza's shoulder.

"Bec!" Eliza smacked Becky's arm.

"What? You've had threesomes before," Becky said.

"Yeah, but not with *Amelia*." Eliza looked back at Amelia. "No offense."

"But she's cute," Becky protested. Amelia didn't know how to feel about that compliment. Somehow it felt more objectifying than flattering.

"Yeah, maybe. But she's like family. It'd be like sleeping with my grandmother." Eliza shuddered.

"And on that note… Goodnight, Becky," Amelia said with a faux smile. As she walked down the hall toward her room, she could still hear Becky and Eliza discussing her.

"You know she used to have a crush on me," Eliza said. "Her failed attempt to flirt is how we became friends in the first place."

"Oh, really?" Becky asked.

Amelia shut the door to her room and turned on her TV, drowning out their voices. Eliza wasn't lying; Amelia had asked her out way back in college. But that was a long time ago. It wasn't as if Amelia was still holding a torch for her. And yet she still felt the light sting of rejection every time it came up.

Amelia flopped down on her bed and zoned out to reruns of The Office. After a few minutes, she could hear the tell-tale rapid thumping and not-so-quiet moaning that told her Becky and Eliza had gotten down to business in the living room. Again. Amelia turned up the volume on the TV and lay down with a pillow over her head.

She must have dozed off because the next thing Amelia knew the house was quiet. Her room was dark aside from the light of the TV, which had stopped auto-playing episodes and was waiting on the 'are you still watching' screen. Amelia rolled out of bed and switched on the light. She opened the door a crack and stopped to listen. There was the soft murmur of the living room television—an insurance commercial—but aside from that were no audible signs of life.

"Please don't let them be sitting on the sofa naked," Amelia whispered to herself as she crept out of her room and down the hall. She got half of her wish. Becky was gone but Eliza was, in fact, sitting naked in front of the TV. She had a blanket on her lap but her pert, round breasts were bared to the world.

"Hey there, Amelia Bedelia," Eliza said, glancing up from the screen. "I was wondering if you'd ever emerge from your fortress of solitude. You hungry? I'm starved."

"I thought you and Becky were going to have pizza," Amelia replied, averting her eyes from her roommate's perky nipples.

"We didn't get around to it. Too busy eating other things, if you know what I mean," Eliza said with a wink.

"She is gone though, right?" Amelia asked, avoiding Eliza's sexual reference and glancing nervously around the house. The last thing Amelia wanted was to get a full-frontal view of Becky coming out of the bathroom or something.

"Yes, relax, she's gone. Apparently, she's got an early morning." Eliza shrugged. If it bothered her that her casual date had turned into a basic booty-call she was doing a good job hiding it; her expression was as perky as her tits. Eliza smiled. "I guess it's just you and me, les-bestie. What do you say? Make us a pizza?"

"I was just going to have salad…" Amelia began. Eliza stuck out a pouting lip and began to whine softly like a puppy. "…but I suppose I could throw in a frozen pizza for you too while I'm at it."

"Thanks, roomie, you're the best."

Chapter 3: Mel

Mel was standing behind the bar refilling a glass of soda when the door to North River opened and the cute girl from yesterday stepped cautiously inside. *Amelia.* She looked nervous—both hands clutching the strap of her backpack, her bottom lip held between her teeth. When Amelia's eyes caught hers, Mel smiled brightly and waved. Amelia smiled back and raised her fingers in a small gesture of greeting before turning and shuffling off to the same back booth she'd sat at the day before. Amelia was wearing a white sweater and a floral skirt that fell just above her knees and swooshed as she walked. Mel watched her slide into the booth and pull out her laptop—the laptop with the rainbow sticker.

Mel was surprised to see her again so soon. She hadn't seemed to like the food all that much yesterday, and she certainly didn't look comfortable there. *She has that rainbow sticker, maybe she's here because of Pat and Nancy.* Mel understood wanting to support local LGBT-owned businesses. But two days in a row? *Maybe she's here to see me again.* The thought made Mel smile. Amelia was pretty; she had soft feminine curves, big green eyes with long dark lashes, and cheeks that dimpled adorably when she smiled. Her chocolate-brown hair had been in a ponytail yesterday but today it was down, the thick waves falling just past her shoulders. She was certainly easy on the eyes, and Mel had enjoyed waiting on her yesterday. The way Amelia had looked at her—her cheeks pink and eyes wide— gave Mel the distinct impression that the attraction ran in both directions. And although Mel was nowhere near ready to think about new relationships, it was nice to think that a cute girl might like her.

"What are you staring at?" Pat's voice behind her made Mel nearly drop the soda gun in surprise.

"What?" Mel asked.

Mel's boss looked across the restaurant to where Amelia sat and then back at Mel, an eyebrow raised in question. "Is that your girlfriend?"

"What?" Mel repeated. "My—oh. No. That's just a customer." Mel set the drink down on the waiting tray and wiped the bar where drops of soda had splattered. "She was here yesterday too."

Pat nodded. "Ah, that makes sense. I thought we might get one or two new 'regulars' this week. With the Dragonfly closed I expect some of those coffeehouse people will be looking for a new place to sit all day on their laptops." She snorted.

"Is it okay if she works here?" Mel asked.

"Did she buy food?" Pat asked back. Mel nodded. "Well, then it's a-okay with me. As long as they get food and don't cause trouble for you and Sebastian, I don't really care if we get a bit of the coffeehouse crowd. And if one of 'em happens to be a cute little lesbian, all the better." Pat winked at Mel. "Just so long as you can stay focused here," she said in a teasing voice.

Mel laughed. "I'll do my best," she said. She looked back across the room toward Amelia. Sebastian still hadn't come out to take her order. On impulse, Mel poured a glass of Diet Coke and walked it over to Amelia's table.

"Diet Coke, right?" Mel asked, setting the soda beside Amelia's laptop. Amelia looked startled but she didn't slam her laptop closed this time, as she had yesterday.

"What? Oh, yes, I do—I mean, thank you," Amelia stuttered. "How did you…?"

Mel gave one Amelia one of her best half-smiles and winked. "I never forget a drink order."

"Thank you." Amelia's cheeks turned that adorable shade of pink again and Mel felt her smile widen.

"I'm at the bar today. Well, I'm at the bar most days, really. That's my post. But Sebastian should be out soon to take your order," Mel explained. "It's good to see you."

"Thanks, I, uh, think it's good to see you too," Amelia said. Her adorable awkwardness made Mel melt a little on the inside.

Don't forget that Pat told me not to get too distracted. Mel reminded herself. With a little wave, Mel turned and went back to the bar and her job. *I'm here to earn money and learn, not to flirt with cute girls.* Mel focused her mind back on customers and food. *Maybe I should try the Rueben today.*

~ ~ ~

Mel got off work early that night and was able to hit the grocery store on her way home. She could practically smell the delicious aroma of the chicken soup she was planning to make as she walked home, her arms filled with delicious and aromatic ingredients. But when she arrived at the apartment, what she found made all thoughts of food fly right out of Mel's head. The grocery bags she'd been carrying hit ground, food spilling everywhere.

"Oh my God."

The apartment had been violently ransacked—everything either stolen or broken. Standing in the doorway, Mel could see that all the living room furniture was trashed. The sofa had been taken, along with the stereo and TV, and the rest had been torn to shreds. White tufts of fluff from pillows and cushions littered the floor. Even the rug was gone.

"What the fuck?" Mel took a few numb steps forward. The kitchen table had been broken in half—it looked as if it had been hit with a sledgehammer. Beyond that all the kitchen appliances had been ripped out.

Mel walked around the kitchen counter and gasped. "Oh shit!" Water was pouring out from the place where the dishwasher had once been. There was an alarmingly large puddle in the kitchen that was spreading out into the rest of the apartment.

"Fuck fuck fuck." Mel searched the ransacked cupboards. The dishes were all gone—many of them in pieces scattered around the wet floor. Most of the good cookware was gone as well but a few pots and pans remained. Mel grabbed the biggest pot she could find and positioned it so that it caught the leaking water. With another, she scooped up as much water as she could and dumped it into the sink. *Towels,* she thought and dropped the pots to run toward the back of the apartment. The linen closet had been emptied onto the floor but at least most of the towels and sheets were still there. Mel grabbed a handful and brought them to the kitchen, desperate to mop up as much of the water as possible.

On some level Mel knew the floors were already ruined, and that she was going to be in deep shit when the landlord found out. But at the same time, she didn't know what else to do but to frantically try and remedy the situation. She fully soaked an armful, dumped it in the sink, and repeated until all the clean towels, sheets, and blankets were sopping wet. She had no idea how to shut off the water, but between the towels, sheets, and the one strategically placed pot, she was able to get the situation under control—at least it wasn't getting any worse.

Mel took a few deep breaths and, after assuring herself the pot wouldn't overflow, she went to see how the rest of the apartment had fared. It wasn't pretty. Whoever had robbed and trashed the place had done so with malice as well as greed. The bedframe was smashed to kindling; the mattress had survived functionally but was covered with muddy boot prints. All of Mel's clothes had been pulled from the closet and dumped into the overflowing bathtub. Even the toilet had been ripped out. Above the sink, on the cracked mirror, written in dark red lipstick read the words, "go to hell, bitch!"

It wasn't hard to guess who'd sacked the place. "Heidi," Mel muttered to herself. "Goddamn it." She was too shocked to be properly angry. *What the hell am I going to do?*

After a few more deep breaths, Mel walked back through to the living room. Everything of value was either gone or destroyed. There were holes in the walls in the living room and along the hallway, but there were no broken windows, and the door was undamaged. Whoever did this didn't need to break in, a fact which only served to further prove her theory that Heidi was behind it all—Heidi had a key.

~ ~ ~

When Mel arrived at work the next day, Pat took one look at her and somehow immediately knew something was wrong. "Are you okay?" she asked, tilting her head in concern. "You look exhausted."

With effort, Mel forced herself to smile. "Yeah, I'm fine." It was a bald-faced lie. Mel had been up almost all night either talking to the police or being screamed at by her landlord. The police had been sympathetic, but they didn't offer her a whole lot of hope that anything would be done with regards to catching and punishing her ex-girlfriend. The landlord had been livid. He'd made it clear that it was one-hundred percent Mel's responsibility to restore the apartment to its previous condition by the end of her lease agreement, or he would not only keep her deposit, but be forced to file against her for any remaining damage.

Mel promised she would take care of it—mostly because she didn't know what else to say. "At least I wasn't kicked out," she'd consoled herself. But the damage was so severe that the landlord was forced to cut off all the water to the apartment. Mel didn't know how long she could manage to live there without running water, but that was a problem she would have to tackle later. Now more than ever she could not afford to lose her job.

"Are you sure?" Pat asked, eyeing Mel suspiciously. "I'm not buying it. Something's up with you."

"I, uh," Mel gritted her teeth and searched for something she could tell Pat. "I had a rough night. My girlfriend… broke up with me." It sounded pathetic, but the full truth was far more humiliating.

Pat put a hand on her shoulder. "I'm sorry to hear that, kid."

"Thanks." Mel couldn't meet Pat's eye.

"Do you need some time off?"

Mel shook her head violently. "No! I need the hours. I'll be fine, really. I just need to wake up." She slapped her cheeks and forced herself to smile again. "I just need a little caffeine."

"You sure? Breakups can be hard." Pat's tone was warm and understanding, which only served to make Mel feel worse.

"No, really, it's fine. I promise you won't find me crying in the ice cooler or anything. I'm used to people letting me down. It's just more of the same, really. I don't need her, but I need this job."

"Okay," Pat said, nodding. "I'll take your word for it. I hate to see such a young person so cynical, but we all have our stuff. I'm glad you can work."

Pat walked off and Mel got down to her prep work. Once North River opened and the steady stream of regulars began to flow in, Mel found she really was able to put her personal issues out of her mind. And when Amelia walked in for the third day in a row, Mel felt genuinely happy to see her. She could use a pick-me-up, and a little harmless flirting was *exactly* the type of pick-me-up to put a smile on her face.

"Hey there, Amelia," Mel said, strolling up to the side of Amelia's usual table.

Amelia looked up; her soft-featured face blushed pink as she stammered out a greeting. "Oh, hi. It's uh, good to see… how are you… Mel?"

She remembers my name. Mel grinned. "Oh, my life's a mess. Tell me about yours, writer-lady."

"I'm not really a writer…"

"Well, I'm not about to call you cheat-for-hire-lady," Mel teased. Amelia's blush deepened and she hunched her shoulders.

"Hey, I'm just kidding around," Mel said apologetically, sliding into the booth across from Amelia. "What are you writing about today?"

"The Byzantine Empire," Amelia replied softly, still looking ashamed.

"Hey, don't be embarrassed. I'm sorry I teased you," Mel said. "Your day job doesn't define you, Amelia. Your passion does."

Amelia looked up from her lap. "Thank you," she said, a sweet smile on her lips. With Amelia's eyes locked on hers, Mel felt her heart skip a beat. Amelia's face was so sweet, like an angel, and the way that she looked at her made Mel feel a warmth beyond the joyful entertainment of a good flirt. Mel was suddenly self-conscious—hyper-aware of how intimate the moment felt.

She cleared her throat. "You'll have to tell me all about it sometime," Mel said, standing up from the booth. "I know absolutely nothing about the Byzantine Empire."

"Yeah, sure," Amelia said. "Any time."

Mel hitched a thumb in the direction of the bar. "Well, I should get back to it. Good luck, Amelia."

"Thanks. You too," Amelia replied. Her voice was soft and sweet, her cheeks dimpling adorably. She was so cute; Mel smiled to herself all the way back to the bar.

~ ~ ~

While Mel was at North River, everything felt okay, almost normal. It was hard living in a shell of an apartment, without appliances or running water, but she was making it work. On the days when Mel opened, she would go in extra early. While she was alone in the restaurant, she would wash herself as best she could using the restroom sink. She got all her meals from North River or one of the takeout places along her route to and from work and did her laundry at the laundromat down the block.

When she wasn't working at the bar, she worked on repairing the apartment. She'd changed the locks and cleared out all the trash. She had a plan, and she was making progress. Days went by and there were no sightings of her ex, but *many* sightings of pretty little Amelia.

As hard as certain parts were, Mel felt like things in her life were on track. At least until the day her landlord called her while she was at work. She'd let the first two calls go to voicemail but when it rang a third time, she got Sebastian to cover the bar and ducked out the back door to the alley.

She answered the phone. "Hello?"

"So you do know how phones work," the landlord barked.

"I'm at work. What do you need?" Mel asked gruffly. She was not a big fan of her unsympathetic landlord these days and, judging by his tone of voice, the feeling was mutual.

"I just had a city inspector stop by. Some asshole must have called him, because he asked to see *your* unit specifically."

"Mine? Why? What happened?" Mel asked.

"A bunch of government fuckery is what," he grumbled. "He says it's unfit for human habitation. I can't let you stay there or I'm going to be slapped with some bullshit fine."

Mel nearly dropped her phone. "What?! I'm being kicked out?"

"Yeah, but like hell am I letting you off the hook."

"Wait, what?" Mel's head was spinning. "What do you mean?"

"I mean you have a rental agreement and you're liable for the damage."

"How can I fix the damage if I can't live there?!" Mel protested.

"You can keep working on repairs during the day, but—"

"I work during the day!" Mel snapped.

"Then hire somebody." The landlord was starting to sound exasperated.

"I can't afford to hire somebody!" Mel said; the whole situation was so unbelievably unfair. But that didn't seem to faze her landlord.

"That's not my problem," he said. "As far as I'm concerned, this a domestic issue and you have to sort it out. I'll expect the rent to keep coming in, the repairs to get done, and no more surprise inspections. Got it?"

"Fine." Mel hung up. She put her back to the brick wall and crouched down. Burying her head in her arms, she screamed in frustration. Everything in her life just seemed to go from bad to worse. Every time she felt like she had gotten her shit under control, it all fell apart again. "What the hell am I going to do now?" Mel screamed again. Angry tears spilled down her cheeks.

"What's wrong?" Nancy was standing at the door. She was a tall, lean woman with shoulder-length dark brown hair with a streak of gray at the front. She was dressed in a charcoal suit and purple blouse. She looked so put-together it made Mel realize what a mess she must look like.

Embarrassed, Mel stood up and quickly wiped away her tears. "I'm sorry. I'll be right back in—"

"I'm not worried about the restaurant. I'm worried about you," Nancy said, putting a hand on Mel's shoulder. "Pat's mentioned you've seemed a little off this week. And we know you've been coming in extra early. What's going on? Is there anything we can do to help?" She took her hand off Mel's shoulder and lit up a cigarette.

Mel shook her head. "It's just…" She ran her fingers through her hair. She couldn't possibly explain it all.

"I, I just got kicked out of my apartment but I don't have the money for a new place," she said. It wasn't a lie and it wasn't as embarrassing as the full truth.

"Well, that really blows," Nancy said, with an exhale of smoke. "But I think we can help you."

"You can?" Mel asked, surprised.

"Yup. I have to make a few calls. Come back to the office on your next break, okay?" Nancy dropped the cigarette and ground it out with her heel.

"Sure," Mel agreed.

Nancy disappeared back inside. Mel took a deep breath, reminded herself to just keep moving, and followed Nancy into the restaurant.

Chapter 4: Amelia

The Dragonfly was closed for the rest of the month, so for the rest of the month, Amelia had no choice but to work from North River. Or at least she told herself she had no choice. It was either that or admit that she was doing exactly what Eliza had predicted she would do: quietly stalk her hot tomboy crush.

She didn't learn much more about the intriguing Mel. She would wave to Amelia from the bar; she even stopped by her table a few times to say hello. But each time Amelia would freeze up and forget to ask Mel anything about herself. Otherwise, Amelia had all her interactions with Sebastian, who was either European, gay, or both, but who never stopped to chat long enough for Amelia to figure out which.

For the most part, Amelia sat silent and alone, doing her work and stealing occasional glances in the direction of the bar. Mel wore a plain white t-shirt every day, her hair always pulled up in either a half-ponytail, braid, or topknot. Amelia couldn't decide which she liked more—they were all hot as hell—although she was dying to see what Mel looked like with her hair loose. It looked silky soft. As she watched Mel from afar, Amelia would often imagine what it would be like to run her fingers through that hair.

The restaurant was quiet; it never seemed to get very busy which—combined with the cozy, cabin-like ambiance—made it very conducive to writing. Despite the beautiful distraction at the bar, Amelia got a lot of work done there. It would have been perfect, if it weren't for the food situation.

Every day Amelia ordered something different off the menu, and every evening she went home and paid the price in stomach cramps and a shameful bloated feeling. And each uncomfortable night was only made worse by Eliza's relentless teasing. Eliza wouldn't have called it teasing, Amelia knew. But she had so many *opinions*, so much 'advice' to impart. She was always sure she could run Amelia's life far better than Amelia did. Amelia knew she should stop giving Eliza ammunition, but she just couldn't keep from gushing about Mel and groaning about the food situation.

Given how much she talked about Mel and the restaurant, Amelia shouldn't have been surprised when her roommate showed up at North River one sunny Friday afternoon. Eliza often took half-days on Fridays or 'worked from home' in the afternoon. And after all the questioning, advice, and comments about 'seeing this supposed hottie for myself,' Amelia should have seen it coming. All the same, when Eliza dropped into the seat across from her, Amelia nearly jumped out of her skin.

"Eliza! What are you doing here?" she exclaimed.

"I came to visit you of course, silly!" Eliza pursed her lips in a wicked smile and looked suspiciously around the restaurant. "So…?"

"So what?" Amelia grumbled.

"So where's the sexy tomboy?" she asked. "I have *got* to get a peek at the *lumberjane* who's got you sporting lady-wood these days."

"Would you shut up?" Amelia hissed. She could see Sebastian on his way to the table.

Eliza took one look at him and raised a critical eyebrow at Amelia. "That is an *actual* boy. You're not changing teams on me, are you?"

"No, now shut up for five seconds," Amelia growled.

"Can I get anything for your friend here?" Sebastian asked.

"No, we're fine," Amelia said quickly before Eliza could answer. Eliza wasn't here for food; she was just here to torture her 'bestie.'

"Okay, I don't get it," Eliza said once Sebastian had gone. "This place is deadski-wedskis. No way they have *two* servers. So where is the mystery lady? Or did…" Eliza gasped. "Did you make her up? Have you been fucking with me this whole time?"

"What? No!" Amelia shook her head. "Why would I do that?"

"Um, maybe to draw attention away from the fact that you've given up entirely?"

"Give up? On what?"

"On life, on love, on yourself." Eliza gestured at her. "Letting yourself go, hiding in the dark, gorging on fried food and fantasies."

Ouch. "I'm not—"

"I mean, I know you've been miserable lately but that's no reason to give up, Amelia," Eliza said in what Amelia assumed she thought was a sympathetic tone.

Eliza reached out and squeezed her hand. "You can turn it around; you've probably only gained five to ten pounds this month—"

"I have not!" Amelia snapped, pulling her hand away. *Have I?* She resisted the urge to touch her stomach; instead she gritted her teeth and stared at her friend. "I haven't given up on myself, Eliza. And Mel isn't a fantasy; she's a bartender."

"Okay, wow listen to you all butt-hurt and serious. '*She's not a fantasy; she's a bartender,*'" Eliza mocked. "If I'm so off-base there's no reason to get defensive, Jesus. You *told* me she was your server."

"She was. But just that first day, when Sebastian was out," Amelia explained, the heat of anger cooling into a sort of frustrated embarrassment.

"So is she here or not?" Eliza asked.

Amelia took a deep breath. "Yes, she's right over there." She gestured discreetly in the direction of the bar.

Mel stood behind the bar wiping down glasses and talking to a couple of guys having drinks. She looked as sexy as ever. She smiled as she talked—a cool, charming half-smile. Amelia sighed.

"So what are we doing sitting *here*?" Eliza popped out of her seat.

"Because I'm— Hey, wait!" Amelia jumped up and grabbed Eliza's arm. "What are you doing?"

"Going to the bar, obviously," Eliza replied.

"But I don't sit at the bar," Amelia said.

"Why not?"

"Because I can't work there. Bars are for drinking—"

Eliza pulled her arm from Amelia's grip. "TGIF, Amelia," she said, flipping her hair back. "Forget work. I want a drink."

"But I have food over here," Amelia protested.

"Oh, so what?" Eliza waved her hand dismissively and looked out across the room. "Oh, hey, server guy?" she called to Sebastian. "It wouldn't be a problem to move her tab over to the bar, would it?"

"Eliza…" Amelia said through gritted teeth, but as usual, Eliza got her way. Sebastian agreed, and the next thing Amelia knew she was following Eliza across the restaurant, her arms loaded awkwardly with her work things and her plate of half-eaten food.

"There, that's better," Eliza said as she perched on a barstool, her face a picture of self-satisfaction.

"I hate you," Amelia muttered under her breath.

"Oh, if you think you hate me now..." Eliza looked down the length of the bar to where Mel was still polishing glasses, and back at Amelia with an impish grin.

Oh no. Amelia felt her stomach do a summersault. *Oh, please don't*, she silently begged, but she knew it was too late.

"Excuse me! Hello? Mel?" Eliza called down the bar. Mel looked over and Amelia immediately dropped her eyes to her lap. She twisted the light floral fabric of her skirt and wished that she were invisible. Eliza was so much—too much. She was going to scare Mel away.

She's going to wreck everything, Amelia thought woefully. *What is there to really wreck, though?* Amelia didn't really *know* Mel, and she would never get to know her sitting quietly watching her from afar. But at the same time, she really, really didn't want Eliza to do this. Unfortunately, it was too late. There was no stopping the Eliza train once it had pulled out of the station.

"Can I help you?" Mel asked Eliza—her voice unusually tight and cool.

Amelia looked up from her lap and her eyes met Mel's.

"Oh, hey, didn't see you there," Mel said, her tone suddenly warmer and more relaxed. "How are you doing, Amelia?" she asked.

"Hi, good," Amelia managed.

"Oh whew! She does know you exist! Bravo, Amelia!" Eliza put an arm around Amelia's shoulder and squeezed.

"And you are?" Mel blinked at Eliza.

"Eliza Cartwright," Eliza thrust out her hand. Mel stared at it. After a beat, Eliza withdrew her hand, seemingly unfazed "Amelia here and I are roommates and long-time les-besties," she said. "It's an absolute *delight* to meet you Mel."

"Les-besties?" Mel repeated, and Amelia wanted to hide under the bar.

"Lesbian best friends! Of course," Eliza explained cheerfully.

"You two are *both* lesbians?" The suspicious tone in Mel's voice made Amelia drop her eyes back down to her skirt. Her stupid, stupid skirt.

"Yup," Eliza confirmed.

"And best friends?" Mel asked.

"The bestest!" Eliza replied brightly. "*Just* friends though, to be clear. She had a crush on me, but we never dated. She reminds me of my grandmother. But that's okay, she got over that crush *ages* ago and now we're…"

"Les-besties?" Mel filled in drolly.

"Exactly!" Eliza perched her elbows on the bar and put her chin in her hands, giving Mel a flirty smile. "Come on, don't sound so shocked, Mel. You've *got* to have heard of les-besties before."

"Can't say that I have."

"But you are a lesbian, right?" Eliza prodded.

"Can I get you something to drink?" Mel asked, evading the question.

"No! Oh no! No way you're straight!" Eliza squealed, sitting back. She squeezed Amelia's hand. "Oh, poor Amelia, not again. I'm sorry, girl." She looked back at Mel. "This has happened before, you know. Poor, Amelia. There was this construction chick—"

"Eliza," Amelia growled.

"It's not your fault, honey. Mel really does look *so gay*—"

"I am gay," Mel snapped. "Okay? Satisfied? Now, either order a drink or—"

"Oh, whew!" Eliza put a hand over her heart and sighed. "That's a relief," she said, smiling at Amelia as if they'd both been on the same page this whole time.

Amelia felt like her brain was about to burst a blood vessel. She stared at Eliza with a mixture of anger and disbelief, but Eliza ignored her.

She turned back to Mel. "In that case I'll have a rye Manhattan, up, with extra cherries," Eliza ordered. Mel looked like she was going to say something but thought the better of it and walked away, shaking her head, to fix Eliza's drink.

"She is hot, oh my God—"

"Eliza, what are you doing? Why did you say all that?" Amelia asked, feeling the burn of tears and bile at the back of her throat. Eliza was making things so wildly uncomfortable. *If she knows how I feel about Mel and she cares about me at all, why is she being like this?*

"To help you, duh!" Eliza said as if it were the most obvious thing in the world.

"You were so… much…" Amelia choked back the threatened tears. "What if she hates me now?" she whispered.

"She doesn't, don't worry." Eliza patted Amelia's knee. Somehow that didn't make Amelia feel any better.

Amelia watched Mel mix the cocktail; the expression on her face was hard to discern.

"One rye Manhattan up with *an* extra cherry," Mel said, placing the drink in front of Eliza, who winked at Amelia before lifting the glass to her lips.

"Mmm, *perfect*," Eliza cooed. "You're an excellent bartender, Mel."

"Anything I can get for you, Amelia?" Mel asked. She was standing right in front of Amelia now, her eyes on Amelia's face as if she were the only one in the room—as if enough fixed concentration could make Eliza disappear. Amelia *wished* Eliza would disappear.

She's not going anywhere. And Mel is waiting for an answer. Say something, Amelia commanded herself. "Uh, um," she stammered. "White wine?"

"What, no! You can't order wine," Eliza scoffed. "Mel can't show off her killer bartending skills if you only order *wine*."

"Oh, well, I…" Amelia began.

"A good bartender gets her patrons what they want," Mel said with a half-smile for Amelia.

Amelia felt her cheeks and chest warm—in a good way, not just in embarrassment this time. *Mel doesn't hate me.* Amelia caught a brief dirty look Mel shot at

Eliza while her 'les-bestie' wasn't looking. *She might hate Eliza...* When Mel returned with the glass of wine, Eliza grinned broadly at her. *Was this Eliza's plan all along?*

"How's the writing business?" Mel asked as she slid the glass toward Amelia.

"Did she tell you she was a *writer*?" Eliza tittered. Amelia felt the burn of embarrassment returning, but Mel ignored her snickering roommate and kept her gaze on Amelia.

Amelia swallowed. "It's going alright. I had a kid tell me I was writing 'too good' the other day…"

Mel laughed. "Too smart for your clientele's own good, huh?" she said.

"Not always." Amelia shook her head. "I have a really challenging assignment I need to finish this weekend."

"I got Amelia Bedelia here hooked up with that gig, did she tell you?" Eliza cut in, apparently bored of being left out of the conversation. She didn't wait for a response. "That story is so crazy, I can't even tell you."

"And yet I get the feeling that you're going to anyway," Mel muttered.

"Mel, you're so funny." Eliza swiped at Mel's arm. "Alright, fine, I'll spare you. I have to use the little girls' room anyhow." Eliza drained the last of her drink and hopped off the barstool.

When Eliza was out of earshot, Mel leaned closer to Amelia across the bar. "I have to tell you something," she said conspiratorially. "I can't stand your roommate."

Amelia grimaced. "She's a lot, I know, I'm sorry."

"So when our date goes well, I'm going to have to insist that we go back to my place, not yours," Mel added. "I'm still settling into the new place, but I think a few unpacked boxes are better company than her."

"Wait. What?" Amelia looked up, stunned. "Our date?"

"Tomorrow," Mel stated. She raised an eyebrow. "Unless you can't get away. I hear you have a very challenging paper to write."

"No, I'm free," Amelia fell over herself to say. "Tomorrow's great. When?"

"I get off at seven, so pick you up around eight?" Mel asked.

Eight? That was a late start to a date, especially for Amelia, who was normally in her pajamas by nine and fast asleep by ten. She was tired just thinking about the concept of starting an activity so late. And yet, she found herself enthusiastically nodding. "That's perfect."

"Great. Give me your phone; I'll put in my number and you can text me your address."

Amelia did as she was told.

Mel smiled when she handed the phone back. "So, I guess I'll see you tomorrow." She slowly backed away from Amelia toward the other end of the bar, her lips curled in a half-smile.

As she went, all Amelia could think of was how badly she wanted to kiss those lips. *Tomorrow. We have a date. Tomorrow.*

~ ~ ~

Mel was the last thing Amelia thought about before bed and the first thing on her mind in the morning. Amelia couldn't remember the last time she'd been so nervous for a date. Eliza thought it was *hilarious*, of course.

"It's adorable how totally freaked out you are," Eliza said as Amelia frantically dug through her closet, trying to figure out what to wear.

"I want this date to go well. I haven't been out in forever and I don't know that I've ever been out with somebody as cool as Mel."

"She is super cool, isn't she?" Eliza agreed. "So cool she's *hot*. Did you see her tattoos?"

"Of course I saw them!"

"Well, you don't need to snap at me."

"I'm sorry, I'm just nervous." Amelia sighed. "She's just so out of my league…"

"She's not out of your league," Eliza said. "You might not, like, *match* but she's not out of your league."

"What do you mean we don't match?" Amelia asked as she pulled on a light floral sundress. *Is this tighter on me than usual?*

"It's just you're all…" Eliza gestured at Amelia. "All girly. Skirts and flowers. She looks like she could be in a biker gang and you look like you're off to high tea. You're like Sandra Dee, scene one, and she's Rizzo." Eliza shrugged. "I mean, it could work. You could be like Betty and Jughead."

"What?"

"Riverdale reference," Eliza said. Amelia stared blankly at her and Eliza pursed her lips. "Yes, I watch Riverdale, don't judge."

"I'm not, I'm not." Amelia put up her hands. She turned and looked at herself in the full-length mirror. The dress was one of her favorites; it complemented her curves; it made her feel pretty. *What good is 'pretty' next to scorching hot?*

She took off the dress and tried again. Jeans and a nice sweater. *I look like a nerd.* She took off the sweater and tried one of Eliza's date-night tops. It was tight, low cut, and basically screamed 'look at my boobs.' *Now I look like a ho.* Amelia must have tried on a dozen outfits before settling on simple jeans and a graphic tee. Eliza didn't approve—not sexy enough—but she did admit that Amelia looked more prepared should Mel pick her up via motorcycle than she had in her little sundress.

"Don't forget that Becky's coming over soon," Eliza reminded her.

"Oh, right." Amelia groaned inwardly. *God, I hope Mel doesn't have to meet Becky.* Mel already didn't like Eliza, and with Becky around, she was twice as bad. Amelia wished the timing had worked out such that she'd be gone for her date by the time Eliza's showed up. She never looked forward to seeing Becky, and she really didn't want to be subjected to her *opinions*—not when she was already nervous about her date.

But Becky arrived in a whirlwind of anger and didn't so much as glance at Amelia. She was seething and ready to throw down with Eliza.

"How is it that I have to find out via *Instagram* that you're dating some chick named Megan?" Becky screeched the second Eliza opened the door.

"Don't get your panties in a twist; I'm not *dating* her. We went out like, twice, maybe three times," Eliza said, waving her hand dismissively.

"Recently?" Becky pressed.

"Why do you care?" Eliza blinked like she was honestly surprised that it mattered at all.

"Did you sleep with her?" Becky asked darkly.

There was a tense moment of silence before Eliza spoke. "We've never said we were exclusive—"

"Answer the question!" Becky snapped.

"In fact, *Becky*," Eliza continued, her voice getting louder with each over-enunciated word. "I believe that I *specifically* told you that I was still dating other people when we got together."

"That was six months ago!" Becky threw her hands in the air.

Has it really been six months already? Amelia did the math in her head. They really didn't act like a normal girl-girl couple six months into a relationship.

"So?" Eliza scoffed.

"So did you sleep with her?" Becky repeated.

Eliza let out a long, exasperated sigh. "We hooked up. Once. It's not a big deal," she said.

Becky's face went crimson. "I can't believe you didn't tell me!" She screamed as she picked up a book and threw it at Eliza. Even though it missed by a good foot, the act was so violent it made Amelia gasp. Her eyes were wide with astonishment as she stared back and forth between the two women.

"I think you need to leave, Amelia," Becky growled.

"Eliza—" Amelia began but her roommate cut her off.

"It's fine. Just go." Eliza nodded toward the door. She didn't need to be told twice. Amelia fled the house for the relative quiet of the front sidewalk.

Amelia took a deep breath. From inside the house she could hear the muffled sound of yelling. After a particularly loud shout followed by a crashing sound, Amelia started to worry for her roommate's safety. She debated going back in but decided to text Eliza first.

'Are you okay?'

The reply came back much faster than Amelia expected. 'I'm fine. Enjoy your date.'

'Ok but text me and let me know how it works out. I can always come back home if you need me.'

'Will do. Thanks, bestie.'

Amelia shivered. The late evening air was cool for summer. She paced back and forth beneath the streetlamp outside the house, sweeping errant twigs and leaves off the sidewalk with her sneakers until Mel rolled up in a black Lyft car. *Not a motorcycle after all.* She waved Amelia over. Amelia double-checked that her smartwatch was set to alert her if Eliza texted before stuffing the phone in her back pocket and climbing into the car with Mel.

"How's it going?" Mel asked.

"Um, good," Amelia mumbled as she buckled her seatbelt. It was dim in the back of the car, but Amelia could see that Mel had showered and changed since work. She was wearing dark pants and a white button-down shirt over one of her usual white t-shirts, and she'd French-braided her hair. She looked amazing and smelled amazing too. Amelia tried to find the words to tell her so, but they stuck in her throat.

The Lyft drove the two of them downtown to a hip little restaurant that made up-scale takes on traditional bar food—burgers and fries with creative twists and locally sourced ingredients. Ordering food made Amelia anxious on dates, so when she saw that they had a

French dip—the dish Mel had suggested at North River the day they met—she ordered it without a second thought. Mel did the same.

"Do you have a taste for those now?" Mel asked when the server left.

"What?" Amelia cocked her head, confused.

"The French dip. When I recommended it, I got the impression that you'd never had one before and since you never ordered it again, I thought maybe you didn't like it," Mel said. Amelia was surprised that Mel had not only remembered the food she'd gotten that first day, but also that Mel had noticed what she'd been ordering since.

"Oh, yeah, no, I like it. I've just been trying—" Amelia's train of thought was interrupted by a text from Eliza.

'I hope you didn't like that cat lamp because Becky may have just broken it. She is so out of her mind angry I can't even talk to her right now but she won't leave.'

'Do you need me to come home?' Amelia texted back.

'No, enjoy your date, I'm just venting!'

My date. Crap. Amelia put down her phone. "Sorry. Roommate trouble. What were you saying?" Amelia grimaced.

"I think you were the one saying something, but I do have a kind of funny story about French dips my boss told me. Remember when people started protesting all things French back in the early two-thousands?"

"Yeah." Amelia nodded encouragingly.

Mel laughed as she recounted her boss's attempts at trolling customers who were so anti-French that the name of a sandwich could set them off. Amelia listened quietly, trying to focus on Mel's words and not to be distracted by either Eliza's texts or Mel's mesmerizing good looks. She felt like she was on high alert—hyper-focused and distracted at the same time. The ball of anxiety building in her chest was almost physically painful. When their meals came, Amelia was still so tense that she barely touched her food.

Why did I order this? Just looking at the meaty monster of a sandwich made her stomach turn. The drama unfolding back at home wasn't doing her stomach any favors either. From Eliza's texts, it sounded like her fight with Becky was on track for breakup town. The whole situation made Amelia tense.

She knew she wasn't being a great date, but she just couldn't seem to string together words in interesting or even coherent ways.

Mel made up for Amelia's quietness, telling her more stories from the restaurant. Amelia was grateful that Mel seemed willing to take the lead for the evening. *I'll do better next time. If there is a next time.*

When they left the restaurant, Amelia expected the night to end—it was already after ten o'clock—but apparently, Mel had more in mind. Amelia didn't want the date to end, exactly, but she wasn't sure she had the energy for it to continue either.

"Where are we going now?" Amelia asked as they made their way through the city, away from the restaurants and clubs, towards what looked like a whole lot of nothing.

"It's a speak-easy," Mel said with a grin. "I've been wanting to go here for a while."

"A speakeasy?" Amelia repeated.

"You know what a speakeasy is," Mel said.

"I do, I've just never been to one," Amelia admitted, stifling a yawn.

"Neither have I. It should be fun." Mel took her hand and led her through an unmarked blue door. Inside, a handful of people were lined up down a long corridor. Mel and Amelia joined the queue. When they got to the front of the line, Mel produced a passcode and the bouncer let them in.

This is like something out of a movie, Amelia thought. She'd never been one for nightclubs, although she'd gone to a few in the past—primarily gay bars, and normally at Eliza's insistence.

The 'secret' bar was absolutely packed. Amelia was immediately overwhelmed. It was warm and dizzyingly crowded. The two of them ordered drinks and stood sipping them at a small high-top table on the periphery of the room.

The tin ceilings, while fashionable, made the crowded bar that much louder. Amelia could barely hear Mel over the din and had to shout to be heard herself. If their conversation at the restaurant had been thin, here at the speak-easy, it disappeared altogether.

They stood together watching the crowd around them, not speaking. Amelia's watch kept buzzing. Eliza and Becky were apparently still fighting.

'Now she's locked herself in the bathroom. I hope the crazy bitch doesn't steal my Xanax!' Eliza wrote.

Amelia drained the last of her drink and sighed. *What am I going to do if I get home and they're still fighting?* She glanced at her watch again. It was almost midnight.

"You look ready to call it a night," Mel said.

"What?" Amelia looked up at her. "Oh, yeah. It's getting late; I should probably get going home."

Mel didn't look happy about that, but she hadn't seemed to be enjoying herself either. She nodded and the two left the bar. The ride home was quiet. Mel hardly said two words and Amelia didn't know how to make it better. Besides which, she was really concerned about Eliza. She hadn't heard from her in a while now, and Amelia was worried about what that might mean.

"Goodnight, Amelia," Mel said when the car pulled up to Amelia's house.

"Goodnight," Amelia repeated. "I'll... see you later?"

"Yeah," Mel nodded.

"Cool, I, uh, thanks," Amelia stammered. With one last little wave, she slid out of the car.

Amelia opened her front door with trepidation. The living room was an absolute disaster. There were books all over the place; her cat lamp lay shattered on the floor—more demolished than simply 'broken'—and every pillow and couch cushion seemed to have been flung around the room as well. *Eliza had better clean this up.* But there was no sign of her roommate—the living room was empty.

Amelia made her way through the house to the kitchen. Eliza was leaning against the counter, a glass of wine in her hand, staring off into space. Her cheeks were flushed and she looked as if she'd been crying.

"Are you okay?" Amelia asked.

Eliza jumped. "Jesus, Amelia, don't scare me like that."

"Sorry, I just got home. Is Becky…"

"She locked herself in the bathroom again," Eliza said bitterly. "Because she's being a sensitive little *bitch*," she added overly loudly.

"I take it you haven't made up then?" Amelia asked. Eliza only scoffed. Amelia put a hand on her best friend's shoulder. "Are you okay?"

Eliza sighed and took a sip of her wine. "I guess. Whatever. Maybe I should have seen this coming. But I just don't even know what she wants now. It's frustrating but I'll get over it. One way or another." She straightened and shook out her hair before turning to give Amelia an appraising look.

"How was your date?"

"Not good," Amelia said flatly.

Eliza arched an eyebrow. "No?"

"I'll tell you about it tomorrow." Amelia was too exhausted to go over it all now. She just wanted to go to sleep. "Any chance you can get Becky out of the bathroom so I can get ready for bed?"

"I can't promise it'll be pleasant, but I'll try."

"Thank you."

Eliza finished her wine before stalking toward the bathroom and banging on the door. "Hey! Time out's up! Amelia is home and needs the bathroom!" Eliza shouted through the door. Amelia watched from a safe distance until Becky emerged, scowling, from the bathroom.

"Well, I'm glad that's over," Eliza said with a satisfied sigh.

"Nothing's over yet," Becky growled.

"Fine. But could we *maybe* not do this in front of my roommate?" Eliza folded her arms.

Becky shot Amelia a dark look before stomping off to Eliza's room and shutting the door with a bang.

"Hey! You can't keep me out of my own fucking room!" Eliza banged on the door.

"It's not locked, idiot!" Becky shouted back.

"Bitch," Eliza grumbled under her breath. She looked back at Amelia. "Good night, les-bestie. Wish me luck."

"Good luck." Amelia waved as Eliza opened the door and stepped into her room. The second it closed behind her the yelling began again.

"Of course I care! Why would I bother fighting if I didn't *care*?!" Eliza's voice was muffled by the door but still perfectly clear.

"You have a hell of a way of showing it!" Becky's voice was louder.

Amelia sighed. *This is going to be a long night, isn't it?*

Chapter 5: Mel

Mel tried to put her failed date with Amelia out of her mind. There was plenty to do to keep her busy. She wasn't opening Sunday, which gave her some time to do repairs at the old apartment. It was easier to do projects now that she had fully moved out and all her things were out of the way.

Nancy had been able to help her find a new place to live remarkably quickly. She had hooked Mel up with a not-for-profit organization that helped young LGBT folks find housing when their families weren't supportive, and they had no other options. Mel almost felt guilty about how easy it had been. She'd told them her story—how her parents had kicked her out, and how her first real girlfriend had taken advantage of her naiveté and gotten her into an impossible situation—and after an impressively fast background check, Mel had keys to a new place.

It was a loft apartment—small but bright, with large southeast-facing windows. Mel had set her bed near the windows, on the opposite side of the room from apartment's small kitchen. The only furniture Mel was able to salvage—aside from the bed—was one lonely kitchen chair, a soft gray ottoman, and a battered-but-sturdy wooden bookcase. Mel promised herself that once she was done repairing the old apartment, she'd put a little time and energy into making the new place feel more like home. For now, she was just glad to have a working shower and a safe place to crash.

Mel worked hard all Sunday, first patching walls at the old place, followed by a closing shift at North River. Life was too busy to worry about cute girls and awkward dates, she told herself. But that didn't keep Amelia out of her mind entirely.

When Monday rolled around, Mel didn't know whether or not to expect Amelia at North River. She hadn't heard from her all weekend. Besides which, the Dragonfly had reopened, so there really was no reason for her to come back. The cost of her meals—which she clearly didn't even like—had to be more than the cost of a coffee at the Dragonfly. *This was only ever just a temporary office for her.*

Mel had fairly well convinced herself that she would never see or hear from Amelia again, so she was taken by surprise when she looked up to see the pretty young woman seated in her usual booth.

"Hey, Sebastian," Mel nudged her coworker.

Sebastian looked up, and then, following her gaze, looked at Amelia. "Oh, she's back," he said. "Didn't you say the date was a bust?"

Mel nodded. "Yeah. If it even was a date. She didn't ever call…" Mel shook her head.

"Did you call her?" Sebastian asked.

"No, I didn't." Mel didn't see any reason to. She'd asked Amelia out; Amelia had said yes but other than that, she hadn't shown any real interest. "Ball's in her court. If she likes me—"

"She'll show up at your workplace?" Sebastian raised an eyebrow.

Mel shook her head; Amelia being there didn't make sense to her. "I guess I should just ask. Mind if I take her table?"

"Be my guest." Sebastian bowed graciously.

With a deep breath, Mel approached Amelia's table. "You're back!" Mel greeted her cheerfully.

Amelia looked up. "Yeah, hi, Mel." Amelia smiled shyly at her. There was an awkward silence.

Come on, Mel thought, *just say what you came over to say.* Mel slipped into the booth across from Amelia. "Hey, so, about the other night… I'm sorry if I misread things," Mel said.

"Misread…?" Amelia looked curiously at her.

"I had thought you liked me, and that the other night was, you know, a date," said Mel.

Amelia blinked, visibly confused. "I do like you; it was a date," she said.

"Really?" Mel asked.

"Of course. Why wouldn't it have been?"

Mel shrugged. She was trying to keep her expression neutral, but inside she was feeling confused as hell. "Because you hardly talked to me, you ate next to nothing, and you dressed so… different."

"What's wrong with how I dressed?" Amelia asked, looking down at herself. Today she was back to wearing the type of thing Mel had grown accustomed to seeing her in: a knee-length floral skirt and light-pink v-neck shirt.

"You were in jeans and a t-shirt," Mel said. "I don't know you that well, but I've seen you more dressed up to sit and work at North River. Like now, you're dressed… cute. But the other night—not that you weren't cute—it just didn't seem like something you'd wear on a date."

Amelia looked down at herself, her round cheeks turning pink. "It was a date," she said softly, not looking up. "Eliza said, and I… I just overthought the outfit."

"But it was more than how you were dressed," Mel hurried on. "You barely spoke to me. It didn't seem like you wanted to be there."

"I'm sorry I didn't talk much. I was nervous…"

"Plus you kept looking at your watch," Mel added, and Amelia hunched her shoulders.

"I'm sorry," Amelia said softly. "I really am." She looked up, her eyes meeting Mel's. "I really did want it to be a date."

"So, what was going on then?" Mel asked. Amelia's words today just didn't match up with her behavior the other night.

"Eliza," Amelia said with a little sigh. "She was blowing up my phone all night. She got in a huge fight with her girlfriend just as I was leaving the house and I made her promise to keep me updated. I'm sorry I was distracted."

Mel still wasn't convinced—if anything, the fact that Amelia, by her own admission, had been thinking about Eliza all night, made Mel more doubtful of the idea that Amelia had wanted to be on that date in the first place. "You didn't have to say yes, if you weren't into it," Mel said. "It's okay. I just thought, after what your roommate said... Do you still have feelings for her?"

"What? No!" Amelia exclaimed, sitting bolt upright.

Mel put her hands up defensively; she'd clearly touched a nerve. "Okay, sorry."

"I really don't," Amelia insisted, leaning forward, her eyes searching Mel's face. "What made you think...?"

Mel shrugged one shoulder. "Well, you did say she was the reason you were distracted. And it gets me wondering if Eliza was kind of bullying you into going out with me. So you wouldn't like her or something."

"What? No. I like you, Mel." Amelia reached out and took Mel's hand across the table. "But... I wasn't sure if *you* liked *me*. I guess part of me kind of thought that it was just a pity date... after the scene Eliza made at the bar."

"I wouldn't have asked you out if I didn't want to go," Mel said.

"Yeah?"

"Yeah." Mel squeezed Amelia's hand once before pulling away and sitting back. "I just don't like games, and I can't stand it when people aren't honest about who they are."

Amelia went back to looking at her lap. "I'm sorry. I was so nervous and distracted… I did everything wrong."

"It's okay," Mel said. "Things don't always work out the way we want. I'm glad I know what happened though. Thanks for being honest." Mel began to stand up from the table, her curiosity about the other night satisfied. "I should probably be getting back to work." Mel stood and began to walk back to the bar.

"I want a do-over!" Amelia all but shouted, stopping Mel in her tracks. She turned.

"A do-over?" Mel asked.

"Yes. Brunch, tomorrow." Amelia straightened her shoulders. "Give me a chance to be myself. I do better in the light of day anyway. So what do you say?"

"I'm supposed to work…" Mel ran her hand over her braided hair and thought about it. *It's an odd day for a brunch date, but what the heck.* "But I can get Sebastian to cover—he owes me one." Mel smiled at Amelia and nodded. "Brunch tomorrow it is."

"Great!" Amelia grinned, the smile bringing out her adorable dimples. "I'll, uh, pick you up at nine?"

"Nine?" Mel winced; if she were to take tomorrow off of work, she would have to swap with Sebastian and close tonight—he hated doing clopens. *He may owe me a favor, but not that big of a favor.* Being up and ready for a date by nine am after closing the night before sounded painful.

"Too early?" Amelia asked.

"A bit." Mel gave her a lop-sided grin. "How about ten, and I'll meet you there. Just text me the place."

"Uh, okay, ten's good," Amelia quickly agreed.

"Great." Mel leaned down and gave Amelia a quick peck on the cheek. "See you tomorrow, Amelia."

Mel sauntered off back to the bar. *She does like me.* The thought made Mel smile. She hadn't realized how disappointed she'd really been about the date until now. She still wasn't sure that she was totally ready to date, but having a cute girl *want* to date her felt pretty good. *It'll be nice to have the attention of a nice woman for a little while,* Mel reasoned.

Normally her workdays flew by, but with the promise of something fun to look forward to tomorrow, the day seemed to drag on forever. She finished the prep work early and puttered around the bar, bored for most of the evening. It was an hour before close and there was only one patron at the bar—the regular, Mark. *He wouldn't mind if I asked him to leave early, would he?* Of all the regulars to ask this of, Mel figured she had a shot with Mark.

"Hey, Mark, can you do me a solid?" Mel asked.

Mark looked up from his drink. "What's that, Melody?" he asked—no matter how many times Mel told him her name was *not* short for Melody, he insisted on calling her that anyway.

"You think you could head on out so I can close 'er up early tonight?"

"Why, you got a hot date?" Mark winked.

"Yup, but it's tomorrow morning and I'd like to get a little sleep."

Mark laughed. "Alright, Melody," he said, his voice rough but warm. "I'll get out of your hair. Just give me a minute to drain the hose, if you know what I mean."

"Alright. Thanks, Mark," Mel said, shaking her head ruefully at his little euphemism. As Mark stumbled off to the men's room, the front door opened.

"Crap," Mel muttered. "Hey, sorry, man, we're closing early tonight." She called across the room.

"Don't worry, this won't take long." The man approached the bar. He was tall with dark hair and a poorly-set nose. It took Mel a minute to recognize him, but when she did, her blood ran cold.

"Brad?"

"Aw, you remembered me. How sweet." Brad, Heidi's husband—the man she'd found in her bed, screwing her girlfriend, the man Mel suspected had trashed her apartment—was standing in *her* bar, sneering at her.

"What do you want?" Mel snapped, crossing her arms.

"I've been looking for you," he said.

"Why?" Mel demanded.

Brad sat casually down at the bar. "Why do you think?"

"No clue, man. You already wrecked my home, stole my shit, and took my girl—"

"She was never your girl!" Brad barked. "She had your number from day one, you stupid backwater bitch. You were just a toy. And experiment. A little fun for her, and a dose of my own medicine for me. She never cared about you."

"Fine, whatever." Mel wasn't about to argue with him. She just wanted him to spit out what he wanted and *leave*. "So why are you here, being a pain in my 'backwater' ass?"

"I want my money."

"What money?" Mel asked.

"The cash," Brad said, leaning forward over the bar. "Heidi gave you cash. I want it back."

"That money was for the rent on the apartment *you* trashed. And it didn't even come close to covering all the damage you did."

That wasn't the answer Brad wanted. He leaned further forward over the bar. "That's my money and I want it back. All of it."

"All of it?" Mel balked. "Dude, it's *gone*." She leaned toward him, doing her best to look calm and assured. "You wrecked the place, took or broke everything, and now you have the audacity to ask for money? Get the fuck out of my bar."

Without warning, Brad's hand shot forward and grabbed Mel by the arm. Yanking hard, he pulled her forward onto the bar top. "You get me that money," he rasped in her ear, "or else I do to you what I did to that shithole apartment." His grip tightened and Mel ground her teeth against the pain. "You got me?"

"You alright, Melody?" Mark's rough voice was like music to Mel's ears.

"Yeah, Mark. Brad was just leaving," she said, glaring at Brad, her heart pounding.

Brad let go of her arm. "I'll be back," he said. "And you'd better have my money." With that he turned and walked out of the bar.

"You alright, Melody?" Mark repeated when Brad was gone.

Mel rubbed her arm and rolled her shoulder. He hadn't done any real damage. "Yeah, I'm alright. Thanks, Mark."

"You sure?"

"Yeah," Mel nodded. "Don't worry, go on home. I'll see you later."

Mark inclined his head to her. "Good luck on your date."

"Thanks." Mel watched as Mark ambled out the door. As the adrenaline from the confrontation wore off Mel felt deep exhaustion weighing on her. She didn't need another complication in her life. It was all so much already. She didn't even have the energy to be as afraid of Brad as she maybe should have been. "Should I even go on that date?" she asked herself. Dragging Amelia into the quagmire of her life seemed unfair. *If we just keep it casual, none of this will have to affect her.*

Mel pulled out her braid and ran her fingers through her hair. She thought about Amelia and felt that little spark of happiness that Amelia lit within her. She didn't want to let Brad—and by extension Heidi—take that away from her. Mel felt she deserved some measure of joy in her life. Brunch with a pretty girl sounded wonderful. *Maybe more than brunch?* Mel mused. *It would be nice to have sex.* She hadn't felt the touch of another woman in so long, and Amelia was so damn pretty. Mel wasn't about to let Brad ruin that. *It's just money. I can figure it out.*

Chapter 6: Amelia

Amelia was brimming with excited energy as she left the house for her make-up date with Mel. Amelia knew the perfect place to take her for brunch: The Highland Café. It was a small restaurant situated above a bookstore near downtown. It wasn't fancy—you ordered at the front and seated yourself; there was no table service. But the food was amazing, especially the breakfast menu. Amelia wouldn't have to worry about what to order or if it would make her sick. She could keep her focus on Mel.

Amelia arrived early and waited outside the street-level entrance. She had stayed true to herself and wore exactly what she should have worn for their first date: her favorite floral sundress. It was a soft pink and fit her curves in flattering ways. She'd pulled her hair into a high ponytail and put on just a touch of makeup. The whole look was a step-up from her day-to-day without being fancy. It suited her.

"Sorry I'm late," Mel said when she arrived, face red from exertion. "It's a longer walk than I expected."

"I'm sorry, I didn't know you were going to walk," Amelia said apologetically as the two climbed up the stairs to the restaurant. "I could have picked you up. I borrowed my roommate's car."

"Don't worry about it, I could use the exercise." Mel brushed it off. "How is Eliza? Still fighting with her girlfriend?"

Amelia shook her head. "No, they made up last night. *Loudly*, if you know what I mean."

Mel laughed. "Does that really mean they're not fighting? Or just that they're also screwing?"

"Touché," Amelia laughed along with her. "I guess I don't really know. They were asleep when I left this morning."

"Is she really your best friend?" Mel asked as they lined up to order.

"Yeah, why?"

Mel shrugged. "From what I saw the other day, it just doesn't seem like she's that nice to you."

"That's just how she is." Amelia shrugged. "She doesn't mean any harm; I think she was actually trying to help me, you know, break the ice, or whatever."

"Break the ice by embarrassing you?" Mel raised an eyebrow.

"It worked, didn't it?" Amelia said casually, fighting against the blush threatening to turn her cheeks red.

"I suppose it did." Mel nudged Amelia's shoulder with her own. "You look beautiful today, by the way."

"Oh." Amelia looked down. "Thanks, you do too," she mumbled.

"Me?" Mel let out a sharp bark of laughter. "Nah."

Amelia looked up at Mel, startled. Mel looked *amazing*, as usual. She was wearing cargo shorts, which hung enticingly low on her narrow hips, and a loose rainbow tank top that allowed a great view of her many tattoos, and just a peek of the gray sports bra underneath. Her hair was tied up in a top-knot and the bottom half looked freshly shaved and indescribably *touchable*. Her face was make-up free and as perfect as always. She was like a lesbian goddess. Just looking at her made all sorts of things inside of Amelia tingle.

"You're really hot," Amelia blurted out and Mel laughed again.

"You're an odd one, Amelia. But I like you." Mel turned her perfect face to the wall-mounted menu. "Now, tell me, what's good here?"

Amelia walked Mel though the menu. Mel ended up with French toast while Amelia ordered a fruit crepe, and they both got mimosas. Amelia led Mel to her favorite table by the window that looked out onto the street below.

"So, uh, the other night you told me that you don't have family in the area, right?" Amelia said as they settled into their seats.

"You were listening," Mel teased with a wink.

"So what brought you here?" Amelia asked, trying to ignore the flush she felt in her cheeks at the reminder of how inattentive she'd been.

"That's kind of a long unpleasant story…" Mel said cryptically as she sipped her drink. Amelia gave Mel her best Bambi-eyed stare until she laughed and gave in to the question. "Well, my parents, I mentioned that they aren't super *thrilled* to have a lesbian for a daughter. I was living there while I was going to college. They'd told me they'd kick me out if they ever caught me with a girl but apparently, video chatting was close enough."

"They kicked you out just for video-chatting with a girl?" Amelia asked, shocked.

"Well, we were a bit… naked," Mel said with a wry smile. "Anyway, I'd been chatting online with Heidi for a while. When my parents lost their shit over the video and threatened to disown me, she convinced me to tell them to go fuck themselves and move in with her two-hundred miles away—here."

"Wow." Amelia couldn't imagine being in Mel's shoes. Her whole family was so supportive of her. "How did that go?"

"You know, growing up, my parents always told me not to trust strangers on the internet." Mel shrugged. "Maybe they were right about that. In my case, anyway."

"So what happened with her?" Amelia asked.

"In short, she broke my heart. It was pretty much a clusterfuck. I'm still digging out from some of that… stuff."

"What kind of stuff?" Amelia asked.

Mel shook her head. "Nah, that's more like a… thirtieth date kind of story," she said.

Amelia was curious but she didn't want to push. A thirtieth date sounded pretty good anyway.

"Suffice it to say, she wasn't really the person she'd led me to think she was." Mel looked at Amelia, her eyes searching Amelia's for something. "That's why being authentic is so important to me," Mel said. "I can't afford to go through that sort of thing again."

"I promise, I am who I say I am," Amelia said, breathless under Mel's intense gaze. "I may not always… articulate myself well, on the spot. But I am me and I won't try to be anybody else."

"Thanks, Amelia."

The way Mel looked at her made Amelia feel warm inside. They were connecting, she could feel it. It was like this really could be the beginning of something special.

"Of course." Amelia smiled.

"Now, tell me about yourself," Mel said, sitting back.

"Like what do you want to know?" Amelia asked.

"Anything, everything. I want to read the book of Amelia…" Mel grinned. "I guess we could start with your last name."

"Fischer."

"Amelia Fischer," Mel repeated, somehow making the name sound way more special that it ever had before. "Amelia Fischer… Any relation to Carrie Fischer?" Mel asked with another wink.

"Oh God, I wish," Amelia sighed wistfully. "She was always one of my personal heroes."

"Mine too," Mel said, sitting up. "Are you a Star Wars fan?"

Amelia shrugged. "I'm not like a super nerd about it, but I did have a crush on Princess Leia as a kid."

"Who didn't?" Mel laughed. "Although I kind of am a 'super nerd' about it."

"Really?" Amelia wouldn't have taken Mel for any kind of nerd. She seemed far too cool for that.

Mel laughed again and held out her arm, forearm up, and pointed to the tattoo there. It was a sort of triangle shape with a strange script written around it. "The Jedi code, written in Aurebesh," she explained, running her fingers across the ink. Amelia's fingers itched to touch that smooth tattooed skin, but she kept her hands in her lap.

"Wow, I guess you *are* a nerd," Amelia teased with a little laugh. "It looks so cool though."

"Thanks." Mel looked Amelia over. "Do you have any tattoos?"

Amelia grimaced. "Just one. It's tiny and *terrible*."

"Yeah? Where? Can I see it?" Mel asked, eyes widening in interest.

"That seems like more of a third date revelation," Amelia said coyly.

Mel grinned back at her. "Is that so? Well, then I hope this second date goes better than our first. Because I want to see that tiny, terrible tattoo."

A warm tingle went through Amelia. "What do you think of our prospects so far?" she asked.

"I'd say signs are good."

The date did continue to go well. The food was good—as expected—and the mimosa helped calm Amelia's nerves. She told Mel all about her family—her parents and sister—about college and meeting Eliza, and about her dreams of one day writing novels for a living. Mel confessed that she didn't read many books but that she loved poetry.

"I write poetry sometimes too, or at least I used to," Amelia said.

"Used to?" Mel repeated.

"I… I haven't written much lately outside of the things I do for money," Amelia admitted.

"Why not?"

"I don't know." Amelia thought about it. *Why haven't I been writing for myself lately?* "Time mostly, I guess. I just feel like it's a waste… Like, any time I could be writing, I could be making money. Writing for the sake of writing feels, I don't know… selfish?"

"I sort of get that," Mel said. "Although I don't see how it's *selfish* exactly. Do you owe that money to somebody or something? Because you know you deserve to do things for yourself too; you don't owe anybody all your time like that."

"No, no." Amelia shook her head adamantly. "It's not like that. I have some school loans, but for the most part I'm trying to save for the future. So I guess it's just… I don't want to let present-me take away from future-me. I want to make sure to give future-me what I promised myself."

Mel tilted her head. "Which is what, exactly?"

"Time off to write. *Really* write. Not like a few hours here or there. I'm trying to save up enough to take a few months off of working altogether—maybe even a whole year—and get my book written." Amelia had been picturing it for years: waking up every day with her laptop and a cup of tea with nobody to answer to aside from her own imagination. It might be an overly romantic idea of what writing was like, but it kept her motivated.

"That's a great goal, Amelia." Mel smiled at her. "I hope you make it."

They wrapped up their meal and walked back down to the street. Clouds had begun to gather in the sky; it looked fairly ominous. Amelia remembered what Mel had said about walking there.

"Let me give you a ride home," Amelia offered. "It looks like it's about to—" A crack of thunder and the sudden start of a tremendous downpour finished her thought for her. "Rain," she squeaked.

Quick-thinking Mel pulled Amelia into the doorway of an abandoned storefront.

"Wow, it's really raining," Amelia said, looking out into the streets where sheets of water pummeled the ground. Mel touched her face, softly turning it until their eyes were on each other. Mel gently brushed a strand of hair from Amelia's damp forehead. The sensation of her fingers on Amelia's skin made Amelia's body come alive with nervous energy.

"I had a really nice time with you today," Mel said softly. "I'm glad you demanded a do-over."

"Me too," Amelia replied, her voice coming out high and breathless. There was a momentary pause—a brief second of questioning hesitation where Mel looked so perfect, so deeply desirable, that Amelia could have cried from longing. *What are you waiting for? Kiss her.*

Amelia wrapped her arm around the back of Mel's neck and pulled her into a kiss. Mel's lips were soft and warm, and they responded to Amelia's kiss immediately. Amelia's insides seemed to melt as they kissed. It was bliss. Heaven. Their lips and tongues moved together in a hungry, ferocious dance. Amelia found that once she'd started kissing Mel, she didn't want to stop. Even knowing where they were—and that passersby might not appreciate the sight of two women making out in a doorway—didn't dampen Amelia's desire.

"Okay," Mel said, pulling away.

"Okay what?" Amelia asked, confused and desperately missing the feeling of Mel's lips on hers.

"Okay, you can give me a ride home," Mel said. "But only if you'll come in with me."

"Deal."

~ ~ ~

Amelia fidgeted with her fingers as she waited for Mel to unlock her apartment door. *This isn't like me. Going to somebody's house after just two dates? What am I doing?*

Mel opened the door and Amelia followed her inside with slow, unsure steps. Mel lived in a small studio apartment. By the looks of things, she hadn't expected to bring Amelia home. For some reason that made Amelia feel better. *This is unexpected for her as well.*

"Sorry about the mess," Mel said as she moved a pile of clothing off of the unmade bed.

"It's okay," Amelia slipped off her shoes and followed Mel into the room, stopping just beside the bed.

Task complete, Mel pulled Amelia close for a kiss and Amelia at once remembered why she'd agreed to accompany Mel home. Her kisses were electric—setting Amelia's body on fire and turning her blood to lava. Urged on by adrenaline and lust, Amelia's base instincts took hold of her actions. Amelia's hands roamed Mel's body with an unfamiliar level of boldness, grabbing at her back, her shoulder, her chest. Mel groaned encouragingly as Amelia pressed her palm against one of Mel's small breasts. Amelia could feel Mel's nipple harden under the thin fabric of her t-shirt and bra.

Mel's hands slid up under Amelia's dress to cup her ass. "You have a perfect butt, you know that?" Mel whispered into her kiss. Amelia let one of her own hands drop to Mel's behind, but she couldn't feel much through Mel's thick cargo shorts.

"Mmm, no fair," Amelia whined, she moved her hand to the waistband of Mel's shorts. Mel pulled back a little and grinned at Amelia—that cool, confident, endlessly sexy grin Amelia loved. She unbuckled her belt and let her shorts drop to the ground with a light thud, revealing tight black trunks. She stepped out of the shorts toward Amelia, and Amelia wasted no time wrapping her arms around Mel and squeezing her ass with both hands.

"Now see, I think *you* have a perfect butt," Amelia purred. Mel's response was to pull Amelia down onto the bed and rolled on top of her. She kissed her again and again as their bodies pressed against one another. Mel pushed one warm leg between Amelia's thighs and Amelia began to moan. She grabbed at Mel, gripping her ass and pulling her tighter against her as they continued to kiss.

"Oh God," Amelia groaned as a burst of pleasure spread warmth and wetness between her legs. It felt so good, but it only served to make her hungrier for more. It had been so long—so very, very long—since she'd had another woman's body on hers, she longed to feel Mel's bare skin against her own.

"Oh my God, just take my fucking dress off," she groaned.

Mel complied with a smile, pulling Amelia's dress up and over her head.

"Now you," Amelia instructed.

"But I'm not wearing a dress," Mel quipped, and Amelia growled. Mel laughed as Amelia pulled her t-shirt and bra up over her head, exposing more sexy tattoos and her two perfect breasts. "I didn't expect you to be so—" Mel gasped as Amelia's mouth found her nipple with her teeth, "—aggressive," she finished, letting out a whoosh of breath.

"Is that okay?" Amelia asked, not fully lifting her mouth away from Mel's addictively perfect nipple.

"Yup," Mel quickly responded.

"Good." Amelia sucked and licked at Mel's nipple while massaging the other breast in her hand. Mel was so deliciously sexy, Amelia could hardly stand it; she was overwhelmed in all the best ways. She wanted to touch every part of Mel, to put her mouth on every exquisitely lickable inch of her skin.

Mel moaned as Amelia flicked her tongue against her nipple again and again. Amelia moved to the other breast, giving it equal attention, until Mel pulled her face up for another series of hungry kisses.

Amelia lifted her hips and let Mel pull off her panties. Mel's fingers traced a path down between Amelia's legs, brushing her clit and dipping lightly into her wetness. Amelia moaned; overcome by need she grabbed Mel's wrist, pushing Mel's fingers deeper inside her. She rolled her hips against Mel's hand. Mel got the hint and began to thrust her fingers in and out harder and faster, rubbing Amelia's clit as she fucked her. Amelia let her head drop back; white-hot pleasure was building. She could see the orgasm coming like the light at the end of a tunnel. She bucked against Mel's hand, rushing toward the light until she reached the end and her whole body was bathed in the warmth of orgasm.

"Oh, God, yes!" Amelia grabbed Mel's hand once again and held it still against her as the waves of pleasure washed over her.

"Did you cum then?" Mel asked, sounding quite pleased with herself.

"Oh yeah," Amelia said with a sigh. She looked wickedly at Mel. "But don't think that means I'm done."

Amelia pushed Mel onto her back and pulled off her trunks. She ran her fingers along Mel's slit, testing for wetness. Mel was wet—*very* wet. She squirmed under Amelia's teasingly light touches. When Mel moved to grab Amelia's hand—as Amelia had hers—Amelia snatched it away and instead lowered herself down to fit her head between Mel's creamy thighs. She separated Mel's labia with her fingers and lowered her mouth onto her clit.

"Oh fuck," Mel breathed. Amelia went to work, licking, pushing, and flicking her tongue on and around Mel's clit. And she loved every second of it: the taste of her, the feeling of Mel's wetness dripping down her chin, the sounds she made. When she came, Mel screamed and clamped her thighs against Amelia's ears. Amelia's tongue darted out for another tiny lick and

Mel's body twitched in response, the pressure of her thighs on Amelia's head tightening.

"So, I take it you're done then?" Amelia asked as she pried herself out of Mel's grip. "Completed your journey, so to speak?" Amelia laughed.

Mel opened one eye to look at her. "Well I would never put it *that* way," she closed both eyes again and sighed, "but yes."

Amelia flopped down beside Mel in bed. "That was really great. All of it. Thank you," she said.

Mel turned to look at her. "You're full of surprises, Amelia."

"Good ones, I hope," Amelia replied, turning to face Mel.

Mel ran one hand along Amelia's bare shoulder. She smiled. "Very good," Mel said. "Very, very good."

"To be honest, I surprised myself too," Amelia confessed. "It's been so long since I had… since I've been with anybody, I was worried I'd forgotten *how*. I certainly didn't expect to take over. I hope that really was okay."

"Yes, it was… perfect." Mel smiled. "It's been a while for me too. And I don't know that I've ever felt such a natural chemistry with somebody before. It was… refreshing. That may not sound like the most romantic way to put it, but it really was great."

"I'm glad." Amelia stared at the ceiling. She too felt refreshed and relaxed in a way that she hadn't in ages.

They lay silently in bed for a while, enjoying the quiet calm and after-sex glow.

Amelia ran a lazy finger along Mel's bare arm, across tattoos, bruises, and bare, perfectly smooth skin. "What would you be, if you could be anything?"

"My boss," Mel said.

"Like, own your own business?" Amelia asked.

Mel sat up on one elbow and grinned. "I was being more literal, but yeah, specifically a business like North River."

Amelia didn't know why this surprised her as much as it did. "You like working in a restaurant?" she asked.

"Yeah, I do. I love seeing somebody enjoy something I made." Mel smiled a far-away smile. "The way people savor a good drink or food is so… personal. I can tell when somebody takes a sip or a bite of something they really like… it's almost *sensual*. Giving somebody something to eat or drink that they really enjoy is… is sort of like giving somebody a good orgasm." Mel laughed and her eyes refocused on

Amelia. "Ironically, now that I've seen you orgasm, I know for sure that I've never seen you eat something you've really enjoyed."

"What do you mean?" Amelia asked, confused. "I've liked the food I've eaten with you."

Mel shook her head. "No, you haven't. Not at North River anyway. At best you tolerate the food there. You don't even like it, much less truly enjoy it. Maybe you liked that crepe this morning—*maybe*… a *little*. But I've never seen you *savor* anything or devour it either. Nothing seems to… turn you on."

"You turn me on," Amelia said. All this talk of food was making her queasy; she'd much rather turn the conversation back to the fantastic sex they'd just had. Amelia flicked out her tongue suggestively. "I like eating you."

Mel threw her head back and laughed. "I won't argue with that." She leaned forward and kissed Amelia. Her kisses were intoxicating. The satisfied feeling inside of Amelia was quickly replaced by renewed hunger and need. She kissed Mel deeper, pulling at her until she rolled on top of Amelia. Mel's thigh was once again between Amelia's and Amelia's between hers. Legs entangled, their hips moved, pressing against one another rhythmically as they kissed.

Oh God, I could do this all day, Amelia thought. And that's pretty much what they did. By the time Amelia said farewell to Mel, she was more tired and happy than she could remember ever having been in her life.

~ ~ ~

When Amelia arrived home Eliza was sitting in the living room reading a book. There was no sign of Becky, much to Amelia's relief.

"How'd things go with Mel?" Eliza asked, looking up from her book.

"Oh my God," Amelia said with a sigh as she flopped down onto the sofa beside Eliza.

"That good, huh?" Eliza raised an eyebrow at her. "Did the 'do over' do *you* over?" Eliza giggled.

Amelia didn't even care that she was teasing. "Oh yeah, there was some doing…"

"So you finally got some, huh?" Eliza tittered. "Been long enough."

"Yeah, and due to being kept up all night last night, I know that you did too," Amelia countered. "So I take it things with Becky are all patched up?"

"More or less," Eliza said with a one-shouldered shrug. "But forget about that. How was it? Mel take you for a good ride?"

Amelia thought back to the afternoon she'd spent naked with Mel. She'd done her fair share of 'riding'—the memory made her smile—but she didn't know that she wanted to give Eliza too many details. Eliza had a hard time keeping her mouth shut, so anything she said could and probably *would* inevitably get back to Mel. And she wasn't yet sure how private Mel felt about things like that.

"We seem to be *compatible*," Amelia said with a coy smile. "She is really hot."

"You aren't going to give me more than that?" Eliza pouted.

"Nope, sorry."

Eliza sighed dramatically. "Fine. Well, you look happy, so *congratulations*."

"Thank you."

Eliza fixed her with a discerning stare. "So, are you two exclusive or do you think she sees other people?" she asked.

"I hadn't thought about it." Amelia fidgeted with a loose strand of hair. "I don't plan to see anybody else. But it's not like we talked about it."

"Well, you should," Eliza said, pursing her lips, bitterness seeping into her tone. "*Trust* me."

"Why? What do you mean?" Amelia asked, looking back at her roommate. Eliza's eyes were suddenly far away, her jaw tight. She looked distinctly *unhappy*.

Amelia put a hand on her friend's shoulder. "What's up, Eli?"

Eliza blinked and shook her head, her gaze refocusing on Amelia. "It's just Becky. That's what the whole damn fight was about. *Exclusivity*. I guess I really hurt her feelings and I never meant to; we'd just never *talked* about it. It's so fucking unfair to act like I broke the rules when I didn't even know…" Eliza shook her head again. "Whatever, it's fine now. I just wish we'd talked about it earlier. We could have avoided a whole thing if she'd just told me sooner what she wanted." Eliza gave Amelia an appraising look. "Don't do that to Mel. She seems like the type who could get pretty much any woman she wants. Don't fool yourself into thinking it's going to be exclusive unless you actually ask, and she actually agrees."

"I, uh, okay," Amelia said, not entirely sure what to make of this bit of advice.

"So you're going to talk to her?" Eliza asked. "Promise me, Amelia. Promise me you'll tell her when you want to get serious. Trust me, if I could hurt *Becky* when she's the strong, self-confident bitch type… Well, if Mel did the same thing to you, I'm pretty sure it would *crush* you."

Ouch. Amelia tried not to physically wince. *I can be strong. I can take care of myself and my relationships, Eliza,* Amelia thought. But she bit her tongue. Eliza was obviously still hurting from her fight with Becky, even if things were all patched up now. Amelia agreed and then let the subject drop. *Even if she said it in a hurtful way, Eliza is right. I should talk to Mel.*

Chapter 7: Mel

Mel was so glad that she'd kept her date with Amelia. She hadn't known how *badly* she needed something positive until she'd gotten it. She wanted to linger in that feeling forever. *I can take the time to enjoy myself a little while longer.*

She'd taken the whole day off from work and although she'd spend the vast majority of it with Amelia, there were still good hours left. Mel knew there were things she needed to do at the old apartment but instead, she made a trip to the grocery store. She hadn't cooked a real meal in her new home yet and she was itching to break in her new kitchen with some culinary experimentation.

Mel put on some music as she started dinner. She couldn't afford fancy ingredients, but that was part of the challenge. If she were to come up with something Pat and Nancy would be willing to add to their menu, it would have to be something simple, delicious, and profitable.

As she cooked, Mel's thoughts drifted back to Amelia. In her mind she ran through the foods Amelia had ordered and the expressions she'd made trying each one. *She likes cheese, but not meat*, Mel thought to herself. *Especially beef.* The only time she'd ordered anything with beef was that first day, when she'd gotten the French dip on Mel's recommendation. Amelia had never touched a burger or steak. Mel could see that she was trying to avoid the deep-fried items as well—she picked at her fried fish last Friday, eating the fish and leaving the crispy battered exterior on her plate. *She's not a vegetarian or anything, but she likes lighter foods.* There wasn't a lot on North River's menu that could be considered 'light.' *Maybe that's what I should be focusing on. If I could add something to the menu Amelia actually liked...*

Mel wasn't sure that the food she was making tonight—a couple fun twists on a traditional grilled cheese—would interest Amelia. They weren't exactly light. But Mel enjoyed making and eating them. The enjoyment she got from cooking and thinking about Amelia, made it even clearer to Mel just how badly she needed to get out from under her troubles with the old apartment so that she could really focus on the things in life she cared about.

Don't care about Amelia too much, she reminded herself. *You're going to keep that casual, remember?* She wasn't ready to get hurt again, she told herself. This was a time for healing and building herself up. *I don't need a serious relationship to be happy.*

~ ~ ~

Amelia walked through the doors of North River the next day—looking fair, sweet, and sexy in a heather-gray dress and cream sweater. Looking at her, Mel couldn't deny the feelings of happiness and desire that Amelia stirred up within her. *I like her more than I'd bargained for, don't I?*

Amelia settled into her usual spot and opened her laptop, jumping immediately into her work. Mel wondered if Amelia had been thinking about her as much as she'd been thinking about Amelia. When Mel closed her eyes, she could still see Amelia's body, taste her lips, and feel her fingertips on her skin. Just the thought sent shivers of excitement up her spine. But from the way Amelia sat in her booth, it seemed like Mel wasn't on her mind at all. In fact, Amelia nearly jumped out of her skin when Mel sat down across the table.

"Hey, cutie. How are you doing?" Mel asked, smiling and trying to look calm and confident.

"Oh, I'm… I'm good, fine," Amelia stumbled over her words.

Why does she seem nervous? Mel wondered. "Do you have something on your mind, beautiful?"

Amelia fidgeted with her skirt. "Can I ask you a question?"

"You can always ask. Can't promise I'll answer," she responded with a wink.

Amelia swallowed and looked up at her. "I was wondering if, uh, we're like… dating? Like dating *exclusively* or…" Amelia shrugged deep into her shoulders and grimaced. "Sorry, that's awkward so early, I just… with what Eliza's been dealing with, with her girlfriend, I just want to be clear that *I'm* not dating anybody else, and I don't plan to. If you are that's… that's fine. I just… I want to, you know, be on the same page."

"I'm a one-woman kind of girl," Mel said with a laugh and another wink. "Don't worry."

"I wasn't worried, exactly," Amelia said, the heat in her cheeks fading. "I just wanted to be… honest."

"And I appreciate that." Mel nodded; the question had been a relief, really. She did appreciate the honesty. But she needed to be honest too; just because she didn't want to see other women, didn't mean Mel was ready for anything serious. And she didn't want Amelia thinking it that meant more than it did. "To that end," Mel said, "I should tell you, I'm not ready to use the word 'girlfriend.' I'm not really in that 'serious relationship' place. But you are the only woman I'm seeing and if anything changes—in either direction—you'll be the first to know."

"Cool," Amelia grinned. "Thanks."

"Speaking of, when do I get to see you next?" Mel asked. "Outside of North River, that is."

"I'm flexible," Amelia replied.

"Oh, I know." Mel winked again.

"Just let me know when you're ready to get off…" Amelia smiled coyly back. "Work, that is."

"Oh yeah, *work*. Sure." Mel threw her head back and laughed. "Well, I've got a few more hours here yet. Why don't you come sit at the bar?"

"Would it be okay for me to do my work at the bar?" Amelia asked.

"Of course." Mel smiled at her. "Unless I'd be too distracting," she teased.

"You might be," Amelia said, closing her laptop. "But it's a chance I'm willing to take."

Amelia gathered her things and followed Mel to the bar. Having Amelia sitting at the bar, talking as they both worked, seemed to bring out the more outgoing side of Amelia. Mel and Amelia really did get along easily once they were both relaxed.

"What are you working on?" Mel asked. "Or should I say, what am I completely distracting you from working on?" she added with a wink.

Amelia glanced at her laptop screen and laughed. "In theory I'm 'polishing' Connor's essay on Foucault and the *longue durée*. But I am having a hard time concentrating." She grinned at Mel. "As much as I like Foucault, you're much more fun. And much more pleasing to look at."

"Oh, but Foucault is such a hottie." Mel fanned herself theatrically.

"No one is as hot as you," Amelia replied.

"Yeah, right." Mel rolled her eyes at the compliment. "Well, don't let my supposed 'hotness' distract you; Conner needs your brilliant help. Besides, I like watching you work. You're cute when you're concentrating."

Amelia's cheeks flushed pink. She looked cute when she did that too.

Sebastian chose that moment to show up at Mel's side. He tapped her on the shoulder. "Hey," he said. "Do you want to take your break? I think there's somebody waiting for you out back."

"What? Um, okay," Mel responded. She was confused for a moment as to who could possibly be waiting for her, but then she remembered Brad's promise to be back and her heart started to pound. *Shit.*

Amelia looked at her, head tilted questioningly. "What's going on?" she asked.

Mel took a breath and shook off her concern; she didn't want Amelia to have even the slightest inkling that anything was amiss. She leaned casually on the bar and gave Amelia an easy smile. "I guess it's time for my break."

Amelia looked disappointed; Mel touched her cheek, stroking her soft pink skin with one finger.

"Don't worry, cutie, I'll be back. Plus, this will give you the chance to get some work done, since I'm so *wildly* distracting." She winked again.

Amelia's eyes were locked on Mel's face; she licked her lips. "Okay," she replied, a little breathlessly.

Mel enjoyed seeing the effect she had on Amelia. The way she looked at her made Mel feel more attractive than she'd ever felt before. "Think you'll still be here when I get back?" she asked.

Amelia nodded and Mel gave her one last little smile before turning and walking through the kitchen out the back. Mel tried to carry herself with the self-confidence she felt when talking with Amelia as she stepped out of the restaurant and into the back ally. As she suspected, Brad was waiting for her.

"What do you want?" Mel asked, crossing her arms, striving to appear irritated rather than scared. Brad looked a lot bigger and more intimidating without the barrier of the bar between them. He was wearing jeans and a tight t-shirt; Mel could see the muscles of his arms tensing as he narrowed his eyes at her.

"You know what I want, bitch. I want my money," he spat.

"I told you, I don't have it," she replied coolly.

Brad took two sudden steps forward, trapping Mel between his body and the brick wall of the building. He was tall and broad, Mel's chin barely as high as his collarbone. He smelled of tobacco and sweat. Mel kept her head held up. "It doesn't matter what you do," she said. "I can't give you money I don't have."

"Then give me the money you *do* have," he demanded. When she didn't comply, he pulled her from the wall. She resisted but he wrapped one long, strong arm around her shoulders, holding her fast, and began to rifle through her pockets with the other. He pulled a small wad of cash from her apron before yanking her wallet out of her back pocket. He let her go, pushing her to the ground. Mel picked herself up while Brad picked through her wallet. There wasn't much cash to be found there, but what he did find, he took before throwing the wallet on the ground.

"Bastard," Mel growled, snatching up the emptied wallet. "You won't get away with this."

Brad's focus snapped back to her and without warning he backhanded her hard across the face. Shock and pain sent Mel stumbling back. She put her hand to her cheek; it had taken the brunt of the blow but the pain in her lower jaw was the worst. She tasted iron and knew her lip was bleeding. She touched it with her hand and winced.

"Not so mouthy now, are you?" Brad said, his face twisted in an evil smirk. "You can expect to keep getting these reminders until I have my money. So unless you like getting your ass beat, I suggest carrying a little more cash on you in the future."

With that, Brad turned and sauntered off, looking remarkably pleased with himself.

"Asshole." Mel spat. She went back inside and immediately grabbed ice and a towel. She looked in the mirror. The whole side of her face was starting to swell. "Fuck." Mel wished she hadn't promised Amelia that she'd be back. She didn't like the idea of Amelia seeing her like this. She took as long as she reasonably could—hiding in back, icing her cheek. The reality of her situation with Brad was starting to sink in.

What the hell am I going to do? Mel lamented. If she was going to be stuck repaying all that money, she wanted to do it as quickly as possible. She was going to need to find ways to cover her other expenses. She considered asking Pat and Nancy for help, but they'd already done so much. And what would she say? *No, I have to take care of this on my own.*

Mel checked her watch. Sebastian would be starting to wonder where she was. With a deep breath she pushed through the doors to the bar. Amelia took one look at her and her eyes went wide.

"Mel, what happened? Are you okay?" Amelia asked, sitting up straight in her seat.

"I'm fine," Mel said with a casual half-smile.

"But your face!"

"Oh, yeah," Mel said, touching her swollen cheek. "Smacked myself pretty good. There's a door in back that sticks. I yanked it. Got myself in the face. It's no big deal."

"Are you sure?" Amelia asked, clearly still concerned. "Your lip is bleeding," she pointed out.

"Thanks." Mel winced slightly as she smiled again. "I wouldn't want to bleed in anybody's drink." Mel picked up a cocktail napkin and touched it to her lip.

"That looks like it really hurts—" Amelia began.

"It's fine really," Mel insisted. She didn't like the way Amelia was looking at her—worry and confusion on her sweet face. She nodded toward Amelia's computer. "How's your work going?" she asked, changing the subject.

"Oh, it's… okay," Amelia fidgeted with the hem of her skirt.

Mel tilted Amelia's chin up. "Hey, I'm okay, really," she said. She searched Amelia's big green eyes for any sign that she believed her. *I am not going to let Brad's bullshit affect my time with Amelia,* Mel promised herself. She wanted to keep these parts of her life separate. Amelia was a pleasure to be with and that's all that she wanted to think about: pleasure. "I'm not closing tonight. Want to meet up after work?" Mel asked.

Amelia nodded, her lips curling into a small, sweet smile. "I would love that."

Mel gave Amelia a quick kiss before Amelia packed up her computer and headed out of North River. When she was gone, Sebastian appeared again at Mel's side.

He looked sideways at her. "You were lying to your girlfriend, right?" he asked.

"She's not my *girlfriend,*" Mel said sourly.

Sebastian groaned. "Fine, whatever. My point is: we don't have a sticky door." Sebastian fixed her with a discerning stare. "That dude back there clocked you in the face, didn't he?"

Mel shrugged, trying to look nonchalant. "We had a disagreement. He's an idiot. It's no big deal."

"You sure?"

Mel shot him a lopsided grin. "I've looked worse."

"If you say so. Your eye's so swollen…" Sebastian waved a hand in front of her face. "Can you even see out if it?"

"Are you being racist?"

"What? No! I didn't say it cuz you're Asian!" Sebastian recoiled and Mel couldn't help but chuckle. He looked so flustered. "It's just… I mean…" he stuttered. "Look at your face!"

"Relax, Sebastian, I was just messing with you. I am aware of what my face looks like. It doesn't exactly tickle, you know." She touched it gently and grimaced. "But it'll be fine, it's just my cheek. Like I said, I've had worse." Mel had picked her share of fights growing up. She'd never really fit in; she didn't really care but she had very little tolerance for those who gave her shit about it.

Sebastian still didn't look convinced. With an exasperated sigh Mel wrapped a handful of ice in a towel and pressed it to her face. "Look, I'm putting some ice on it. Happy?"

Sebastian shrugged. "It's your face."

~ ~ ~

Several hours later, Mel left work and met up with Amelia. She'd been tense for the rest of her shift, but her stress began to melt away with the first kiss Amelia gave her. They wasted no time; they went directly to Mel's place and stumbled into bed together amid a flurry of hungry kisses. After half a dozen orgasms, Mel was so relaxed she could almost forget about Brad and the money entirely. In a way it didn't even feel real; it felt like it belonged to somebody else's life. Her life was filled with warmth and sex and hope; there was no place in that life for fear or desperation.

Amelia lay on her stomach in bed next to Mel, looking as happy as she could ever remember seeing her.

"Oh, there's that third-date tattoo," Mel said, her fingers dancing along the skin of Amelia's lower back, tracing the lines of the lily tattooed there.

"You didn't see it last time?" Amelia asked.

"No, I guess I was more focused on your front-side." Mel grinned; she *liked* Amelia's front side.

"I forget it's there most of the time. It's not like I can see it without a mirror," Amelia sighed. "I wish forgetting about it made it disappear. It's embarrassing."

"Why is it embarrassing?" Mel asked, her fingers moving over Amelia's lower back in slow circles.

"Because it's a 'tramp stamp?'" Amelia scoffed and rolled over to her side, forcing Mel's hand to slide onto her hip instead. "Because it's every type of terrible cliché for a first tattoo?"

"Aw, did you get it for a girlfriend?" Mel teased. One look at Amelia's face and Mel knew she'd inadvertently hit a bullseye. She couldn't help herself and began to laugh out loud. "Oh my God, I was joking. Did you really?"

Amelia groaned and buried her face in Mel's shoulder. "Maybe," she muttered.

"Don't be embarrassed," Mel said, wrapping her arms around Amelia and pulling her closer until Amelia's head rested on her chest. "I have some embarrassing tattoos too, you know."

"What? No way, your tattoos are all so cool," Amelia protested.

Mel let out a bark of laughter. "No, they really aren't," she insisted, snickering. "Look." Mel sat up and pointed to her right ankle and the small pink heart with the now illegible scrawling text across it.

"What's it say?" Amelia asked.

"Forever Yours," Mel replied. "Luckily I was smart enough not to put her name on it, not that it matters since you can't even read it." Mel laughed to herself and shook her head. "Oh well. Maybe I'll cover it up with something else someday."

"How many tattoos do you have?" Amelia asked, her eyes traveling the length of Mel's body.

"Oh, I can't even count anymore," Mel said.

"What does this one say?" Amelia's fingers brushed along the inside of Mel's right bicep. Mel lifted her arm so that all the words could be easily read, but she recited them anyway. "*Come what come may Time and the hour runs through the roughest day.*"

"That's Shakespeare," Amelia said, clearly surprised.

"I am aware." Mel laughed. "It's from—"

"Macbeth." Amelia grinned.

Mel was impressed. "You really are smart, aren't you?"

"And you really are a nerd." Amelia kissed her. "But still the coolest nerd I know." She kissed her again. "What made you get that particular line?" Amelia asked.

"I'm a bit of a collector of the 'shit happens' genre of quotes and sayings," Mel said. "Or at least I used to be."

"Used to be?"

"I'm trying to shift toward taking responsibility for how I handle said shit." Mel looked at the ceiling. "*It's not what happens to you, but how you react to it that matters*," she intoned.

"That seems like a good philosophy." Amelia tilted her head. "What prompted the shift?" she asked.

"It's a funny story, sort of. I was in a pretty dark place when I first moved here, away from my family. For the longest time I didn't even have a job, all I had was Heidi." Mel shook her head, shaking away thoughts of her ex-girlfriend. "Anyway, while I was applying for jobs, I started cooking more at home. I was just sort of figuring out how much food and cooking meant to me. One day I was trying to find a recipe on *Epicurious,* and because I'm a terrible speller, I accidentally ended up reading about *Epicurus* instead. He was a Greek philosopher who had this focus on simple pleasures…

And for whatever reason that quote—*it's not what happens to you, but how you react to it that matters*—struck a chord. I decided it was time to stop blaming every bad thing in my life on the universe dumping on me and try to focus on working with what I have." Mel smiled wryly. "That philosophy has been tested something hard lately, but I still stand by it. I want to enjoy the pleasures of life. I don't want the bad things to control me."

Amelia smiled at Mel. "Cooking is for you what writing is for me," she said. "That's your passion."

"Yeah, well, I'm still working on what that means in the long term. I don't have a concrete plan or anything. I like your plan to save up so you can take a year off and write a book… I just don't know what the equivalent path is for me." Mel shrugged. "But I'm trying to make the best of the little things each day and figure it out along the way without getting bogged down by the hard stuff. If that makes sense."

"It makes sense." Amelia softly touched Mel's cheek and Mel tried not to flinch. Although the swelling from earlier had gone down, it was still sore. She knew Amelia wanted to know more about the 'hard stuff,' but

Mel wasn't ready to share that. That was part of the beauty of separating Amelia from all that.

Amelia ran her fingers along the tattoo. "I like it," she said.

"I like *you*." Mel leaned forward and kissed her, and Amelia kissed her back. Mel let herself be carried away in Amelia's kisses once more—all the while reminding herself to be grateful to the universe for bringing her this thoughtful, amazing, sexy woman to balance out all the dark bullshit.

Chapter 8: Amelia

Amelia spent nearly every free moment she had with Mel. During the day she would work at the bar, and at night she and Mel would be up until all hours exploring one another's bodies.

Amelia returned home one morning, after a wonderful late night with Mel, and found Eliza in the kitchen. They hadn't really seen much of each other all week, and if she was being honest, Amelia hadn't really missed Eliza all that much. It was nice to have some time and space with Mel without her roommate's opinions and advice. Although Eliza's advice about asking Mel about exclusivity *had* been good, and Amelia had to admit that she sort of owed Eliza for pushing her to talk more directly to Mel, that didn't mean she needed daily doses of her 'wisdom.'

"Hey, Eliza," Amelia greeted her cheerfully.

"Hey, roomie. Nice walk of shame. Had some good times with the bar babe, I take it?" Eliza replied with a hint of bitterness.

Amelia ignored the 'walk of shame' comment and sat down next to Eliza at the kitchen table. "Guess what?" she said.

"Chicken butt," Eliza replied through a mouthful of cereal.

"Mel has a Shakespeare tattoo." Amelia thought that would be of particular interest to Eliza. And she didn't know why but Amelia felt compelled to show her roomie how Mel was so much more than just a 'bar babe.'

"Shakespeare?" Eliza lifted an eyebrow suspiciously. "Oh? What is it?"

"*Come what come may. Time and the hour—*

"*Runs through the roughest day*," Eliza finished. "A bit bleak and cliché. Very fitting for an emo-biker-type though, I suppose."

Amelia sighed. "You're so judgmental." *So much for impressing Eliza.*

"I don't judge," Eliza scoffed.

Amelia rolled her eyes. "Except when you do," she said drolly.

"True." Eliza smiled and gave Amelia a little one-shoulder 'sorry-not-sorry' shrug.

"Well, I still think the tattoo is cool." Amelia stood up and began to make herself a cup of tea. In her mind's eye she could see her fingers tracing the all the tattoos decorating Mel's soft skin. The thought made her squirm. She sighed. "She's got so many cool tattoos, all over her arms and back and chest… they're so *sexy*."

"Ugh, don't talk about *sex*," Eliza whined. "I'm far too horny."

"Where's Becky these days?" Amelia asked, realizing she hadn't seen or *heard* Becky all week. "I thought you two'd made up?"

Eliza sighed theatrically. "We did, in theory, but I think she's like… testing me or something." Eliza stood and dropped her bowl in the sink with a clatter that made Amelia cringe.

"It's utter bullshit," Eliza grumbled. "She hasn't been '*in the mood*' for like, ages, it feels. And I can't even go get that itch scratched elsewhere! It's like she wants *my* cake and to keep me from eating it too." Eliza crossed her arms and leaned back on the counter, pouting like a petulant child.

"So, you think she's still punishing you?" Amelia asked.

"I don't even know. She *claims* she's over it and that her little libido dip is purely coincidental…"

Amelia sipped her tea and examined Eliza's posture. She was acting angry, but she almost looked *worried*. "But you're not buying it," Amelia stated. "Is there something you think she's not telling you?"

"What would that be?" Eliza snapped. "Are you insinuating that she—"

"I'm not insinuating anything." Amelia should have known better than to ask questions. Eliza hated being questioned or appearing vulnerable. "I was just making conversation. But I have a lot of work to do so—"

"Wait," Eliza sighed. "I'm sorry for snapping. I'm probably just PMSing or something. You know how I get."

Amelia did know, but she also knew better than to agree that Eliza seemed pissy. "I really do have a bunch of extra work, but I can hang out for a while, or even maybe watch TV or something while I do it, if you want company."

"Why do you have so much extra work?" Eliza asked.

"I took on another couple clients."

Eliza looked sideways at her, eyes narrowed. "Why though?" she asked.

"I've been talking to Mel a lot about my ultimate goal. You know, of writing my own novel one day." Amelia chose not to notice Eliza's eye-roll. "…and I guess it's got me feeling a little more motivated to make money faster so that I can get there. I have the time—"

"Oh yeah, because *time* isn't something new relationships require at all," Eliza muttered sarcastically, rolling her eyes again. "If you have so much time, why not start writing your *novel* now?"

Amelia hated the way she always said *novel*, like she never in a million years could believe her friend capable of writing something worthy of the label. *Not that I have done anything to prove otherwise.* Amelia sighed. "I'm just not ready to commit the time I want to yet. I want to do it right. Really put my heart into it."

"Just so long as you're not avoiding it."

"I'm not."

"And so long as you can stay on top of all those clients," Eliza added. "Remember, that work can stack up fast come finals," Eliza reminded her unnecessarily.

"I know, I know." Amelia took her laptop and sat down in the living room. "Now do you want to turn on the TV, or do you want me to tell you about my latest assignments?"

"Anything good?" Eliza sat down beside her. "Or like, entertainingly bad? I'm always up for another *totally original* take on Chaucer by a nineteen-year-old frat boy. A treatise on sticking one's ass out a window, perhaps?"

"No," Amelia laughed. "No Chaucer. Would you settle for the fascinating history of educational reform during the Meiji restoration?"

"I'll pass, thank you."

~ ~ ~

Eliza wasn't entirely off-base in her concern over Amelia's ability to juggle her new clients and relationship. Amelia found her days at North River were becoming less and less productive each week. But they were also more and more enjoyable. It was worth losing a couple of clients and earning a bit less money, because she was with *Mel*. And from what Amelia could tell, Mel seemed to feel the same.

"Hello, beautiful," Mel greeted her when she sat down at her new regular seat at the end of the bar. "You look lovely today, as usual." She grinned at Amelia and Amelia grinned back.

"And you look sexy, as usual," she said quietly before leaning forward for a quick peck. Mel did look sexy. Her hair was braided, her face bright. She'd rolled up the sleeves of her t-shirt exposing more of her strong, tattooed arms. Amelia ran her fingers along Mel's arm and bit her lip. Touching Mel—even as slight of a touch as that—could make Amelia squirm in her seat.

"Hey look, Melody's pretty girlfriend is back," Mark, one of the bar regulars, called from the other end of the bar. "Hello there, pretty girlfriend," he greeted her.

Amelia dropped her hand from Mel's arm and waved at Mark. He'd been introduced to her by name several times, but he insisted on calling her 'pretty girlfriend,' and when Mel didn't object, Amelia decided that she liked it. She and Mel had been seeing each other for a month now. She was ready to be thought of as Mel's girlfriend.

"What would you like to eat, pretty girlfriend?" Mel asked and Amelia felt like Mel had been reading her thoughts. *She wants me to be her girlfriend too.* She beamed at Mel, her heart swelling.

"Whatever you want to bring me," Amelia replied. Mel had made it her life's mission to find something on the North River menu that Amelia would *love* to eat. Amelia didn't really care for the food, but she did love the attention, and it seemed to matter to Mel, so she continued to try each dish brought to her.

"I'll be back in a bit," Mel said before disappearing into the kitchen. Amelia pulled out her laptop and scrambled to get a little work completed while Mel was busy. These days, any time Mel didn't have patrons to serve or prep-work to be done, she would spend that time on Amelia. They spent so much time talking, Amelia could no longer count on getting an appreciable amount of work done while at North River. But she did what she could when Mel was busy, and crammed the rest in over evenings and weekends when Mel was working.

"Here, try this," Mel said, sliding a steaming bowl covered with melted cheese in front of Amelia.

"What is it?" Amelia asked, sniffing at it.

"French onion soup." Mel grinned. "It's one of my favorites here. Have you never tried French onion soup before?"

"No… but it smells good." Amelia poked at it, trying to figure out how to get at the broth below the crust of cheese. Mel watched her with a look of amusement as she excised a spoonful of cheese, bread and broth. Amelia blew on the steaming hot food before bringing it cautiously to her lips. It was hot and salty and tasted of beef and onion; it wasn't bad. It didn't taste as heavy as a lot of the other food she'd had at North River. *My stomach might even accept this.* "It's good," Amelia said, after a few bites.

"Yeah, but you don't love it." Mel sighed, visibly disappointed.

"Sorry," Amelia conceded.

"No, don't be sorry." Mel shook her head. "I guess I really just have to cook for you myself. Honestly, I can't believe I haven't done that yet. I guess I keep getting distracted by… other things when I'm around you. Sorry about that."

"It's okay, really," Amelia assured her. "I like 'other things.' Besides, we haven't really been dating for that long yet."

"It feels like we have," Mel said. "In a good way," she hastened to add.

"I agree," Amelia said. "And actually… This may sound juvenile, but you know, today is our one-month anniversary."

"It is, isn't it." Mel smiled.

"So, I have a little something for you." Amelia unzipped her bag and reached inside.

"You didn't have to do that," Mel began to protest, but Amelia shook her head.

"It's not like a real gift or anything, I just…" Amelia pulled out a piece of paper and held it out to Mel. "I wrote you a sonnet."

"You wrote me a sonnet?" Mel repeated, her eyes wide.

"It's not anything really." Amelia could feel herself blush. "It's just… you told me you liked poetry, and I'm rubbish at modern poetry, but since you like Shakespeare and I've spent a lot of time being 'beaten up by the Bard' that—"

"What?"

"Oh, that's what I call it when Eliza tries to win arguments by quoting 'the Bard.'"

Mel shook her head. "Have I ever told you that you and your roommate have the oddest relationship?"

"I believe you have." Amelia grinned. Mel had done a fairly good job avoiding Eliza in person over the past month, but she couldn't avoid hearing about her. Amelia's life was just too intertwined with her best friend's. Amelia hoped that the stories she told would endear Eliza to Mel—Eliza was an important person in her life, and she wanted Mel to be a part of that life. Amelia's feelings for Mel had been growing stronger day by day. That's why she'd written the sonnet; she wanted to tell Mel how she really felt.

Amelia thrust the paper forward across the bar. "Uh, anyway, yeah, I wrote you a sonnet. Here."

Mel didn't reach for it—only shook her head. "Oh no, Shakespeare is meant to be performed, not read."

"It's not Shakespeare; I wrote it," Amelia protested.

"I'm sure it's just as good."

"It so very much is not." Amelia shook her head.

"I still want you to read it to me. Pretty please." Mel looked at her with her sweet, dark eyes and Amelia had no choice. She felt her cheeks burn as she held the paper in front of her and cleared her throat.

"When first my eyes did fall on you,
I knew that I would never forget your face.
That you would look favorably on me too,

I did not expect such could be my place.

You gave me a second chance to be true to me,

And as myself to make you mine.

Forever grateful, I will be

For that extra bit of time.

You are cool, like a crisp clear night

And like the stars, as hot as fire

Your body, the world's most welcome sight

But your mind awakes my most deep desire

Please now take these lines to heart,

As you have mine, shall we not part."

Amelia set down the paper, and with heart-pounding trepidation looked up at Mel. Mel's expression was unreadable, her lips pressed close together and her eyes still locked on Amelia's face. Without a word, Mel walked around the bar.

"Where are you—" Amelia thought she was leaving but Mel circled back and pulled her into a deep kiss.

"So, you liked the poem?" Amelia asked breathlessly when their lips parted.

"Very much so," Mel responded. Her fingers brushed Amelia's face, pushing stray hair away from her eyes and tucking it behind her ear. Amelia shivered as Mel's fingers traced her ear then down along her jaw.

"Do you mean it?" Mel asked, her eyes on Amelia's mouth as her thumb stroked Amelia's bottom lip. "What you said in the sonnet?"

"Of course. I wouldn't have written it if I didn't," Amelia replied, her voice tremulous.

A small smile crept over Mel's lips. "Good," she said in a voice so soft it was almost a whisper. "Because you have my heart too." She looked up, her eyes meeting Amelia's. "I think I'm falling in love with you," she said.

Amelia's heart seemed to stop. "Me too," was all she could manage before Mel kissed her again. Warmth radiated out from Amelia's chest as she kissed Mel back. The moment was blissfully perfect—magical— but far too short-lived.

"Excuse me," Sebastian's voice cut through, breaking the spell. "Mel, I hate to be a wet blanket, but you, uh, have *somebody* waiting for you out back…"

Mel's body stiffened. The warmth disappeared from her expression and was replaced by something cool and detached.

"What it is?" Amelia asked.

"Nothing," Mel said sharply. "I have to… I'll be right back." Mel hurried past Amelia and Sebastian toward the back door of the restaurant.

"Do you know what that's about?" Amelia asked.

"Not really," Sebastian shook his head. "A guy comes around now and then. It *never* puts Mel in a good mood. But I haven't the foggiest idea why and she won't tell me. Sorry."

Amelia sat at the bar, unsure what to do while she waited for Mel to return. She checked the time. It was later than she usually stayed at the bar. When Mel did return, she looked shaken up. Her movements were jumpy, her body language tense. Her hair, which had been neatly braided, was disheveled and falling into her face. Mel noticed Amelia's appraising look and quickly fastened it into a top knot.

"Sorry about that, Amelia," Mel said. She seemed flustered and distracted as she tied on her apron. "I have to get some stuff done around here. I assume you're heading out soon?" Mel began to shuffle things around in the bar, moving glasses, wiping surfaces, her shoulders hunched. Her hands may have been shaking; it was hard to tell, she was moving so fast.

"Uh, yeah." Amelia stood and began to awkwardly pack up her things. "I just have to close my tab."

"Don't worry about it. My treat," Mel said. "Consider it an anniversary gift."

"Oh you don't have to—"

"Amelia," Mel said. She stopped and put down the glass she'd been drying. She took Amelia's hand across the bar and gave her a small lopsided smile. "I love you," she said.

"I love you too," Amelia replied.

Mel gave her hand a firm squeeze. "I'll see you tomorrow. Text me before you go to bed?"

"You don't have any time tonight?" Amelia asked.

"Naw, sorry. I have to close, and I know that's past your bedtime." Mel gave her hand another squeeze before resuming her work with the glasses. "I get off early tomorrow—maybe we can hang out? Like, get a pizza and watch a movie or something?"

"That would be perfect," Amelia agreed. "I'll talk to you later then."

"Later." Mel nodded. "Bye, Amelia."

"Bye, Mel."

Chapter 9: Mel

Mel watched Amelia leave, a pit in her stomach. Brad's visit on her 'anniversary' with Amelia had brought home to her the reality of how divided her life had become and how untenable that was. Mel took Amelia's sonnet out of her pocket and unfolded it.

Please now take these lines to heart,

As you have mine, shall we not part

Mel had been surprised but deeply touched by Amelia's words. Mel hadn't expected or planned on telling Amelia she loved her. She wasn't even sure she'd really known herself until Amelia had read the sonnet, her voice so nervous but sincere. It had made Mel's heart swell in her chest. And in that moment, she knew, despite her attempts at keeping things 'casual,' Mel had fallen for Amelia.

If Mel really did want things to work with Amelia—which she did—she needed to get Brad off her back.

Brad had seemed ready to be done with her too. When Mel had handed over her latest installment, Brad had been visibly disappointed. He'd tried to give her an ultimatum; Mel had explained she was already giving him the money as fast as she could and no threat he could make would cause more money to magically appear. That had pissed him off more. Luckily, he hadn't done much more than shove her around, but he'd made it clear: he wanted the rest of the money and he wasn't willing to wait much longer.

"You know, one of these days dealing with you isn't going to be worth it anymore and I'll just fucking kill you. So you'd better hurry the fuck up and get me my money. For both our sakes," Brad had said. He wanted the rest within the week, but Mel knew it was going to take at least a month.

She didn't really think Brad would *kill* her—at least that's what she told herself. But he could still really hurt her. He had the strength and the complete lack of morals necessary to beat the ever-living hell out of her. And she didn't really want that to happen. As tough as Mel was, she was still human and the thought of what could come next scared her.

Mel looked at the paper in her hand. *What would Amelia do if I ended up really getting injured? I would have to tell her then.* Mel's heart hurt thinking about it. She ran her fingers along the lines of the sonnet.

> *You gave me a second chance to be true to me,*
> *And as myself to make you mine.*
> *Forever grateful, I will be*
> *For that extra bit of time.*

If anything did happen, Mel hoped Amelia would give her the chance to explain—although Mel wouldn't entirely blame her if she didn't. Mel had made a big deal about wanting Amelia to be honest and show her true self; but Mel was the one keeping secrets. She was the one hiding part of her life from the person she cared about. *I'm doing it to protect her,* Mel reasoned. *This situation doesn't define who I am. It's temporary.*

"You know, she knows something's up," Sebastian said, snapping Mel out of her thoughts.

"What?" Mel quickly pocketed the poem.

"Your girlfriend—she is your girlfriend now, isn't she?" he asked.

"Yeah," Mel admitted. "She is."

"So if you really like her, you should probably tell her what's going on with that dude that keeps coming by." Sebastian was looking at her disapprovingly.

Maybe he was right, but she wasn't ready to give in. She was still holding out hope that she'd find a way to get rid of Brad before Amelia found out. The whole situation was incredibly embarrassing. Amelia was crazy smart; she would never let herself get stuck in a situation like this. It would be mortifying for Mel to admit to just how stupid she was to end up in such a mess.

"It's nothing. I just owe him some money, is all," Mel said. "It's not a big deal and I'd rather just pay him back and get it done with."

"Why do you owe him money?" Sebastian asked.

"None of your business," Mel snapped. "Forget I mentioned it."

"Have you thought of asking Nancy and Pat for help?" Sebastian suggested.

Mel shook her head. "No way."

"Why not? Wouldn't you rather owe them than some dude who beats you up?"

"He doesn't beat me up," Mel said tersely. "And I can take care of myself."

Sebastian put his hands up. "Fine. Do whatever you want. But you should know, your North River family has your back. And I think your girlfriend would too if she knew what was going on."

Mel didn't know what to say. She turned and began stacking glasses to wash. She had learned long ago not to rely on help from others. The whole situation with Heidi had just hammered that lesson home.

She loved Amelia, and she loved her 'North River family' but she had to do this on her own. To involve them would be to put her relationships with them in jeopardy, and she wasn't willing to do that.

I could have a real future here, and with Amelia. I am not going to mess that up.

Chapter 10: Amelia

When Amelia returned home and opened the front door, her ears were met with the sound of Eliza's whimpering tears. Amelia dropped her bag and stepped further into the room. Her roommate was sitting, curled on the sofa, surrounded by crumpled tissues. The tip of her pointed nose was pink, and her eyes were red from crying. Amelia immediately went to sit beside her on the couch.

"What's wrong?" she asked, looking Eliza over. Although it was early evening, Eliza was already dressed in her pajamas. Something was seriously amiss.

"Becky broke up with me." Eliza sniffed. "For good. For real."

"Oh, Eli, I'm so sorry." Amelia put a hand on Eliza's shoulder, but she shoved her off.

"No, you're not! You hated Becky! You're probably *happy* that she dumped me!" Eliza snapped before her tears overtook her.

Surprised, Amelia sat back. While it was true that she'd never liked Becky, she didn't hate her as much as she hated seeing Eliza hurt; surely her best friend had to understand that.

"I'm not happy to see you upset," Amelia said softly. "I'm sorry I didn't get along with her… I just… I didn't know she meant so much to you."

"That's because you never wanted to hear about her! You never took the time to really get to know her!" Eliza yelled through her tears.

Amelia couldn't help but bristle at Eliza's sharp tone. "Did she leave you because I didn't like her?" Amelia asked.

"Of course not," Eliza huffed. "It had nothing to do with you."

"Then why are you yelling at me?"

"I'm just upset, okay?!" Eliza shrieked.

Amelia gritted her teeth. She didn't deserve to be hollered at just because she happened to be the one around when Eliza was feeling bad, but at the same time she felt for Eliza. Being dumped was never fun—even if it wasn't the love of your life. Just because Amelia thought Eliza was better off without Becky in the long run, that didn't mean Eliza didn't have a reason to hurt now.

There was a knock at the door. Eliza buried her head in her arms and moaned. "It's her. She wants her stuff."

"Becky?" Amelia looked at the door.

"Who else?" Eliza growled. "Can you just… deal with her? I can't even look at her stupid face." Eliza stood up and—wiping away her tears—stomped off toward the bedrooms. Before Amelia could say anything, Eliza slammed the door closed—shutting herself inside *Amelia*'s bedroom.

"Great. Just great." Amelia sighed to herself as she made her way to the front door. The second she opened it, Becky burst through. "Come on in," Amelia mumbled under her breath.

"I won't be long," Becky said over her shoulder as she marched toward Eliza's room. "Where is the selfish *twat*, by the way?"

"She's not a selfish twat and she's not here," Amelia lied. She followed Becky to Eliza's room to keep an eye on her as Becky threw things into a couple of cloth shopping bags. "What happened?" Amelia asked, despite herself.

"I just couldn't take any of her shit anymore." Becky turned to give Amelia an appraising look. "I don't know what she did to get you to be so *complacent* about her fuckery."

"What? I'm not… What?" Amelia stuttered.

Becky rolled her eyes. "She just always has to have it her way, you know? It took so long to get her to stop fucking *cheating*. And once she finally stops messing around, then suddenly I'm not 'worth it' unless I make her the center of my goddamn world? It's such bullshit."

"Wait, I thought you dumped her," Amelia said, confused both about what had happened and why she was talking to Becky about it.

"I did!" Becky threw up her hands. "She was up my ass all the fucking time! Like just because I don't want her fucking around with other girls doesn't mean I want her attached to me like a goddamn wart." Becky disappeared into the closet and came out with a handful of clothes.

"Hey, that's hers." Amelia pulled a coral sweater out of Becky's hands.

"How do you know?" Becky snapped, yanking it back.

"Because I gave it to her!" Amelia snapped back. She'd had quite enough of being yelled at for one day. "Just get your stuff and get out of our house."

"Whatever," Becky muttered, tossing the sweater back at Amelia. She picked up a couple more items before storming out. When the door shut behind her, everything felt very quiet and still.

"Eliza?" Amelia opened the door to her room. Eliza was curled on her bed facing away from the door. Amelia stepped into the room. "She's gone."

"Good." Eliza sniffed but she didn't stir from her spot on Amelia's bed. Amelia sat down beside her and put a hand on her back.

"It's going to be okay, you know," Amelia cooed. Eliza grabbed her hand and pulled her closer. Amelia curled up behind her roommate and hugged her.

"She's right though," Eliza whispered.

"What do you mean?"

"I am a selfish twat."

Amelia squeezed her. "You are not."

"Yes, I am." Eliza sighed. "I know what I am, and I know that I'm a lot."

"I know you're a lot, that doesn't make you a… twat," Amelia said. She didn't say Eliza wasn't selfish.

She couldn't truly say that. Eliza *was* selfish. But it was part of who she was. And with the right people that was okay. Clearly Becky wasn't 'the right people.' "Becky never brought out the best in you," Amelia added. "I think you can do better."

"Thanks." Eliza hugged Amelia's arm. "And thanks for putting up with all my 'fuckery.'" Eliza turned her head. "You know, you really can hear like, everything going on in my room from here."

Amelia laughed. "Oh, I am *well* aware."

"I'd offer to trade—you can't hear a thing from my room—but I guess I'm too selfish." Eliza sighed.

"I'd never ask you to. It's not how we work."

"But we do work?" Eliza asked. "Les-besties forever?"

"Les-besties forever," Amelia confirmed.

~ ~ ~

Amelia didn't realize until the next morning that she'd never texted Mel last night as promised. With all of Eliza's drama, Amelia hadn't even plugged in her phone—it was completely dead. *Mel's probably still asleep now anyway.* She left the phone charging and went to make herself a cup of tea.

Eliza had originally dozed off in Amelia's bed, but at some point, while Amelia was still sleeping, she had left for her own room. Or at least Amelia had assumed Eliza had gone to her own room. She was surprised to find her sleeping on the sofa in the living room. Eliza stirred when Amelia walked past.

"Hey."

"Hey. What are you doing sleeping out here?" Amelia asked.

"My bed smells like her," Eliza groaned. "The whole room does. I just want to burn it all down."

"Please don't." Amelia smiled at Eliza but she just continued to look miserable. Amelia sat down by her feet. "Come on, it'll be okay. Wash your sheets, burn a candle, or maybe some sage—you know, cast out the demons of the old relationship. It might make you feel better."

Eliza sat up. "Would you do that for me?"

"Me?" Amelia blinked at her.

"Please." Eliza gave Amelia one of her patented pouts.

"Okay. You go shower, I'll get those things started."

"Thank you, bestie." Eliza went off to shower and Amelia got to work, stripping the sheets from Eliza's bed, loading them into the washer, and digging out a few of her own scented candles to scatter around the house. By time she was done, Eliza was out of the shower. Amelia showered as well before joining Eliza in front of the TV.

"Feeling any better?" Amelia asked.

"Marginally." Eliza sighed. They watched TV in silence for a while as Amelia tried to brainstorm ways to help Eliza get over Becky. She couldn't remember the last time Eliza had taken a break-up so hard. Usually the shoe was on the other foot. Eliza dated a lot but hadn't had many serious relationships. *Is that why I didn't realize she was serious about Becky?* Amelia had fewer relationships, but in almost all of them she'd fallen in love. Although never as fast and hard as she was falling for Mel.

"Mel!" Amelia jumped off the sofa. "Shit."

"Oh my God, you scared me!" Eliza whacked her on the leg. "What's going on?" she called after her as Amelia rushed to retrieve her phone from the bedroom.

"I was supposed to text her last night, then my phone was dead this morning, and I totally didn't," Amelia explained. "I hope she's not mad…" Amelia looked at her phone. There were several texts from Mel.

Amelia wiped a hand across her face. *I suck.* She felt so guilty for making Mel worry. She texted back—a long rambling text explaining Eliza's situation and about how her phone had died. And then she apologized profusely.

Mel responded quickly. 'It's okay, I'm just glad you aren't upset.'

'I'm not upset. I love you,' Amelia replied.

'I love you too.'

'So, when can I see you?' Amelia texted back.

'How about brunch tomorrow? I'll cook.'

Amelia frowned. She'd expected to get to see Mel today. *Is she mad about the texts?* Amelia typed out another text. 'Not today? I thought you got off early.'

'I was supposed to but I have to take care of some things so I'm actually working until close. I'm sorry. But I promise I'll make it up to you tomorrow.'

'Okay, no worries. I look forward to tomorrow.' Amelia set down her phone and then picked it up again. 'Is it okay if I visit you at work today?'

'Always, beautiful.'

Amelia smiled. She glanced at her roommate, sitting zoned out in front of the TV. Eliza still looked mired in a storm cloud of her own unhappiness; a trip to the bar could do her some good.

"Hey, Eli. Come with me to North River," Amelia said.

"Why?" Eliza raised an eyebrow.

"Mel has to work; I want to say hi. And you really look like you could use a drink."

Eliza sighed. "I can't argue with you there. Okay, let's go."

When Amelia and Eliza arrived at the bar, Mel was prepping garnishes.

Mel's face lit up when she saw Amelia. "Hey there, beautiful," she said.

"Hey, sexy," Amelia replied quietly, feeling her cheeks burn as she did. Mel did look as sexy as ever, in her white t-shirt with hair pulled back—hair Amelia now knew *was* silky soft. "It's good to see you."

"Ditto."

Eliza groaned, drawing Mel's attention to her presence.

Mel's expression cooled noticeably. "Hello, Eliza," she said dully.

Eliza leaned closer to Amelia. "I just got dumped, could you *please* not throw your relationship in my face right now?" she snapped in a loud whisper.

Amelia felt her blush deepen. "Sorry." She didn't like being snapped at, but she saw Eliza's point. *Of course being with another couple would be uncomfortable for her right now.*

Across the bar, Mel rolled her eyes.

Amelia gave Mel a pleading look and Mel sighed. "Something I can get you ladies to drink?" she asked with professional politeness. "Rye Manhattan up with extra cherries?" Mel looked at Eliza.

"Long Island," Eliza replied coolly, not acknowledging Mel's impressive ability to remember her dink order from over a month ago.

"Coming right up. And for you, my dear?"

"She'll have the same," Eliza answered for Amelia. Mel looked questioningly at her.

"I guess I'll have the same." Amelia shrugged. "It's kind of our traditional drink-away-our-problems drink."

"Ah, the break-up," Mel nodded. "How are you doing with that?"

"The time has come, the walrus said, to talk of other things," Eliza replied darkly.

Mel didn't respond but began to make the drinks in silence.

"I'm sorry if you didn't want me to tell her—" Amelia began.

"Of shoes and ships and sealing wax, and cabbages and kings," Eliza continued raising her voice.

"Eliza—"

Eliza only got louder—she was half-way to shouting now. "And why the sea is boiling hot and whether fish have wings."

"Okay, okay, new subject," Amelia acquiesced. Several bar patrons were staring at them now. *What, haven't they ever seen a heartbroken lesbian loudly reciting Alice in Wonderland in a bar before?* Amelia sighed. "Anything interesting going on at work these days, El?"

"As a matter of fact," Eliza dropped her voice back to a reasonable conversational volume as she began to tell Amelia about a case she was working on. Eliza relaxed as she chatted and drank. She seemed to take pleasure in annoying the hell out of Mel, but Mel was a good sport about it. *I should remember to thank her tomorrow.* Amelia and Eliza left the bar before dinner, because Eliza 'couldn't even imagine eating any of the so-called food there.'

"I've seen you get sick from this place one too many times, Amelia Bedelia. And we only have the one bathroom, you know," Eliza reminded her, a little too loudly, as they walked out.

"Okay, fine, we're going," Amelia said with a sigh.

"Thanks, bestie," Eliza put an arm around Amelia's shoulders. "You can cook me something when we get home."

Chapter 11: Mel

Mel had told Amelia that she wouldn't be available today, but watching her walk out of the bar with Eliza hanging all over her sparked feelings of jealousy within Mel. She didn't like Eliza, and the fact that she got to go home to Amelia every day added a note of bitter envy to her already negative feelings regarding Eliza.

The better Mel got to know Amelia, the more clearly she could see all the different ways Eliza toyed with her. Eliza had gotten Amelia her 'cheating for hire' job, but it was clear enough that Eliza made her feel bad for taking it. Eliza picked at Amelia's relationships too; the story she liked to tell regarding Amelia's past crush was just the tip of the iceberg. It was clear as day to Mel that Eliza liked Amelia's attention. She wanted Amelia to pine for her—it made her feel powerful.

Mel had the sudden terrifying thought that if Eliza was distraught enough about her breakup with Becky, that she might actually try something with Amelia. Mel could easily picture Eliza's gloating face if she managed to break up their relationship, only to reject Amelia again. Mel couldn't shake the thought once she'd had it.

I have to see Amelia tonight. Mel knew she wouldn't relax until she had Amelia in her arms again. By the time she came to this conclusion it was somewhat late, but she took a chance and texted Amelia anyway.

'Are you asleep?' she asked

'Not really,' Amelia texted back.

'Think you can stay up until I get off?'

'After close?'

'Yeah. If that's too late I understand.'

'No, it's okay. I can stay up… but would you be willing to come over here? I'm already in my PJs.'

'Any chance I can sneak in without Eliza noticing?' Mel did *not* want to see Eliza, or Eliza to see her.

'Oh yeah, she's passed out in her room. I'll leave the front door unlocked so you don't even have to knock.'

'Great! See you in a couple hours, beautiful.'

Mel's shift crawled by. The second the drawers were pulled and doors locked, Mel ran out. It was almost three in the morning by the time she crept into Amelia's house. She'd only been inside once before; Amelia had given her a brief tour one evening when Eliza wasn't around. They'd been rushing out to catch a movie, so Mel hadn't had the time to give the place a good look, but she'd seen enough to be familiar with the layout, even in the dark. By the light of the moon, Mel made her way through the living room, and past the kitchen to where Amelia's bedroom door stood ajar.

Amelia's room was bathed in a soft, pink light emanating from the Himalayan salt lamp on her dresser. Amelia was in bed, wearing nothing but panties and a t-shirt. She was asleep—her hair splayed about the pillow. The light of the lamp made Amelia's brown hair look auburn and her cheeks pink—as if she'd been in the sun all day. She looked so peaceful and incredibly beautiful.

Mel closed the door behind herself before pulling her t-shirt off over her head. It smelled of sweat and fried food—all of her did. There wasn't much to be done about it, though. Mel stripped down to her trunks and climbed into bed beside Amelia.

Amelia stirred as Mel drew her into her arms.

"Mel?"

"Shhh, you're asleep," Mel cooed softly.

"I'm not anymore," Amelia protested.

Mel softly stroked her hair. "You can go back to sleep, it's okay. I just wanted to be with you."

"I don't want to go back to sleep," Amelia said.

"Why?" Mel asked.

Amelia squeezed Mel tight. "I think I was having a bad dream," she said quietly.

"About what?"

Amelia only shook her head. She pulled back until she was looking into Mel's face. She touched her cheek. "I love you," she whispered.

A shiver of joy ran through Mel. "I love you too." Mel kissed her. Amelia's breath was minty, like she'd brushed her teeth not long ago. Mel kissed her deeper, searching for the taste of Amelia beyond the toothpaste. Amelia kissed her back with hunger. Mel let her hand run up under Amelia's shirt to lightly cup one warm breast. Amelia gasped when Mel's thumb brushed across her nipple. The sound of Amelia's reaction and the sensation of her soft flesh in Mel's hand sent a ripple of pleasure through her. Mel pushed unconsciously closer to the beautiful woman she held.

Mel broke their kiss momentarily to pull off Amelia's t-shirt before pulling her close again. She ran her hand down along Amelia's ribcage, over the soft curve of her hip, and around to her ass. She squeezed, pulling Amelia's hips tighter against hers. Amelia really did have an amazing ass. Mel hummed in pleasure as Amelia's body pressed against her, their legs intertwining. When Mel slipped one of her legs between Amelia's soft thighs, she felt Amelia roll her hips, her mound rubbing against Mel.

Mel slipped one hand between their bodies, inside Amelia's panties, until she felt Amelia's clit pressed against her fingers. Amelia moaned encouragingly and continued to roll her hips. She was panting now; the sounds of Amelia's pleasure made Mel breathless with desire. Her own body throbbed and she opened her legs slightly further until she could feel the weight of Amelia's leg on her. She pushed against Amelia as Amelia continued to ride her hand.

Mel slipped her fingers deeper between Amelia's legs and felt the wetness there. "Oh, God," Mel moaned. Feeling Amelia's slick opening caused the wetness between her own legs to grow. Mel pushed two fingers inside of Amelia.

Amelia groaned and shifted her weight, pushing Mel's fingers deeper within her. "Oh yes," she sighed as she began to thrust against Mel's hand.

Mel forgot about her own desires entirely as she watched Amelia, entranced. Amelia looked like a goddess in the faint rose-colored light, sweat making her flushed skin shine like polished stone. Her supple breasts bounced as she moved; Mel reached out and lightly touched one pink nipple, brushing it with her fingertips before tracing the round underside of Amelia's breast.

Amelia whimpered and Mel looked up at her. Her eyes were squeezed shut in concentration. *She's close*; Mel could tell. Mel watched Amelia's face as she crossed that invisible line. When Amelia came she threw her head back and let out a cry of pleasure.

"Oh my God," Amelia said breathlessly. Her chest was heaving. She collapsed against Mel. Mel could feel her racing pulse as she kissed Amelia's neck.

"You are so damn sexy when you come, you know that?" Mel whispered in her ear.

Amelia laughed. "Yeah right."

"I'm serious," Mel insisted. "You're sexy as hell. Here." Mel took Amelia's hand and guided it into her trunks, between her legs so that Amelia could feel just how wet she'd made her. "See what you do to me?"

"Mmmm," Amelia purred. "Good. I like turning you on." She began to spread Mel's wetness in slow circles around and over her clit. Mel relaxed into the bedding as Amelia touched her. She was so incredibly turned on that it didn't take long before the crescendo of pleasure peaked and she came, moaning and shaking.

"Oh God, Amelia..." Mel sighed. "You're amazing." She pulled Amelia into her arms and kissed her. "I love you."

"I love you too," Amelia replied sleepily.

Mel yawned; she too was feeling the pull of sleep. "Sweet dreams, Amelia," she whispered before falling into a deep, dreamless sleep.

~ ~ ~

When Mel woke up in the morning, Amelia was no longer in bed with her. Sun was shining through the slats in the blinds. Mel checked her watch. It was already after nine. *Shit*. Mel was supposed to be at work by eleven. She climbed out of bed and looked around the room, trying to locate her discarded clothes. She found her t-shirt on the floor. She picked it up and sniffed it. *I can't wear this*, she thought to herself. She sniffed under her arms. *And I need a shower*. She groaned. She didn't know how she was possibly going to get home, shower, and still make it to work on time. *Double shit.* Mel pulled out her topknot and ran her fingers through her hair.

"I love when you do that," Amelia said from behind her and Mel turned. Her girlfriend was standing in the doorway, two steaming hot cups of coffee in her hands. She shut the door behind herself and handed Mel one of the mugs.

"There you are," Mel said, accepting the mug. "Hey, would you mind if I used your shower, and maybe borrowed a t-shirt? I'm running really behind this morning; I have to be at work before the lunch shift," Mel explained.

"Of course." Amelia leaned forward and planted a soft kiss on Mel's lips before setting down her coffee and opening her dresser drawer. "Will this work— Oh!" Amelia stopped. She was looking at Mel with sudden concern.

"What?"

"Your back..." Amelia lightly touched Mel's shoulder blade.

"What about it?" Mel asked, craning her neck to see what Amelia was pointing to.

"You have some big bruises along your back. Didn't you know?"

Mel shrugged. "No, I didn't know."

"What are they from? They look painful," Amelia said.

Mel shrugged again. She knew exactly what they were from. The last time Brad had paid her a visit, he'd shoved her so hard against the brick wall of the building that the blow of her back against the unforgiving surface had knocked the wind out of her. It was no surprise that the impact had also left bruises. But she wasn't ready to tell Amelia about all that, so she feigned confusion.

"No idea. But it doesn't hurt, so it doesn't really matter. Come here." Mel pulled Amelia close and kissed her deeply. Amelia hesitated a moment before kissing her back.

"Are you sure you're okay?" Amelia asked when the kiss was over.

Mel gave her a lopsided grin. "I'm okay. But I'd be *fantastic* if you'd agree to join me in the shower."

"You don't have to ask me twice." Amelia grinned back. "I'll go get us some towels."

Mel wrapped the towel Amelia gave her around herself; it was soft and pink and was so very *Amelia*. She loved that. She followed Amelia out of her room to the bathroom.

"Ooh, did you get a booty call, Amelia Bedelia?" Eliza's voice sent a ripple of irritation through Mel. She scowled.

"Ignore her," Amelia said under her breath, pulling Mel into the bathroom and shutting the door.

"You horny little girl," Eliza called through the door. "Don't worry, I won't listen in!" she added.

"She really knows how to ruin the mood," Mel grumbled.

Amelia ducked her head. "Yeah. Sorry."

Mel took Amelia's head in her hands. "Hey, it's not your fault." She kissed her and Amelia smiled. "Besides," Mel added. "I probably shouldn't take too long. I really do need to get to work on time."

"Do you still want me to go in with you?" Amelia asked. "The shower I mean."

"Of course, beautiful." Mel kissed her once more before they got down to the business of showering. Hyperaware of Eliza's presence just outside the door, Mel couldn't relax enough to do much in the shower other than wash and kiss. But it was wonderful nonetheless.

When she got out, she braided her hair and put on the green v-neck t-shirt that Amelia had offered her. Other than the shirt, she still wore all her own clothes.

"Do I look presentable enough?" Mel asked.

"You look great. Green's a good color on you," Amelia said.

"Well good, because this is going to be a long shift, I should try to look halfway decent to start it off." Mel grinned at her girlfriend.

Amelia frowned. "A long shift? Are you closing again?"

"Yeah," Mel confirmed. "And I think I ought to go home after. I have some things I need to get done… But I can probably see you tomorrow." Mel was expecting another visit from Brad tonight. She knew she didn't have all that he wanted, and she knew that he was going to be angry. She didn't need Amelia seeing her right after whatever retribution Brad decided to dish out.

Amelia looked disappointed, but she nodded. "Tomorrow's good for me," she said. She touched Mel's arm and smiled at her. "I'm so glad you came over last night. That was… wonderful."

"I'm glad I came over too. And that you came… over me." She winked.

Amelia's smile broadened, her adorable, dimpled cheeks turning pink.

"Have a good day, Amelia," Mel said. She gave Amelia one last kiss and left for work grinning widely. *Today is going to be a good day; I can feel it.*

Chapter 12: Amelia

Amelia had thoroughly enjoyed Mel's late-night visit. She was tired, but it was worth it. The only thing about Mel's visit that didn't make Amelia smile was the memory of the bruises across her back. Not only did they look painful, but the sight of them had triggered a memory: a dream. After seeing the bruises, Amelia could suddenly and vividly recall the dream she'd had about Mel: the dream Mel had interrupted when she showed up in person—the nightmare Mel had saved her from.

Amelia tried to push the thoughts away. *It was only a dream.* She had other things to do today. Not only did she absolutely have to get her latest assignment out today, but Amelia had promised Eliza that she'd spend some time with her. Eliza was still visibly hurting from her breakup. She needed one of their classic les-bestie girls' nights in.

When Amelia's work was done, she made dinner for both her and Eliza, which they ate in the living room in front of the TV. Amelia tried to stay focused on her friend and the show they were bingeing, but she still couldn't stop thinking about Mel. No matter how many times she told herself the dream was just a dream, she still couldn't shake the weird feeling growing in her gut. She kept picking up her phone to ask Mel about her bruises, and putting it back down again, question unasked.

"Okay, what's going on with you?" Eliza asked after a few such false starts.

"Nothing," Amelia lied.

Eliza scoffed. "Don't give me that. You've been in your head *all day*. I know something is on your mind. Spill it." Eliza fixed her with a stern look.

"I think Mel might be hiding something… Something… dark." Amelia confessed.

"What makes you think so?" Eliza asked, sitting up.

"I don't know… Something just isn't sitting right." Amelia twisted her hair. "I had a dream last night."

"And so did I." Eliza snorted softly to herself. "You can't base anything off a dream."

"Sometimes you can dream things true," Amelia pointed out.

"Are you fucking with me?" Eliza raised a suspicious eyebrow.

"What?" Amelia didn't follow but clearly Eliza didn't believe her.

Eliza rolled her eyes. "Okay, I'll play along. You say sometimes you do dream things true? Then I say, I see Queen Mab hath been with you."

When the reference hit home Amelia rolled her eyes. "I'm serious, Eliza," she said, throwing a pillow at her roomie. "I'm not doing a bit. Any resemblance to Romeo and Juliet is… coincidental."

"Well, I hope so," Eliza said, throwing the pillow back. "Because otherwise you've cast me as Mercutio, apparently, and I'd prefer not to die, hurt under your arm, or in any other way."

"I don't know why I try to talk to you about anything." Amelia started to stand, but Eliza reached over and pulled her back down.

"Come on, wait," she said. "What *outside* of your dream makes you think she's hiding something?"

"She's had a couple odd bruises and injuries she can't—or won't explain. And the other night there was this guy… She said it was nothing, but the look on her face… I don't know. Something is going on."

"If you have all that why would you bring up a fucking *dream*?" Eliza squinted at her.

"I didn't connect the things together until I noticed her back today…" Amelia shrugged. "I still have no proof that there is any connection, but in my dream, the man was hurting her. He was like, her secret husband. I know that was only a dream but…"

"But what?"

"What if her ex—the one she told me lied to her—what if that was actually a guy and he's still harassing her or something? What if she's still secretly seeing him?" It sounded silly but the thought put a knot of anxiety in Amelia's gut.

"I thought you asked her about being exclusive," Eliza pointed out.

"Yeah, and what she said was that I'm the only *woman* she's seeing. Technically she didn't say she wasn't seeing a guy too."

"You think she's secretly straight and in an abusive relationship?" Eliza whistled. "That'd be one hell of a secret," she said.

"I don't think the dream is *that* true," Amelia said, fiddling with the hem of her shirt. "I just think there might actually be a connection. Something is up with her and this guy."

"So, let's find out what it is," Eliza said, sitting up straighter. She had a look in her eye that told Amelia she already had an idea.

"How?" Amelia asked.

Eliza leaned forward and lowered her voice conspiratorially. "Stake her out," she said. "Follow her. See if she sees him again. And if she does, find out what they're *doing*."

"That doesn't seem like the right way to go about it…" Amelia frowned. "I should just talk to her, ask her about it."

"So ask. Text her." Eliza leaned back and crossed her arms.

"I've been trying to," Amelia protested. "But I can't think of what exactly to say."

"How about 'what are you hiding?'" Eliza suggested.

Amelia shook her head. "No way. That would sound so blunt and accusatory—especially as an out-of-the-blue text."

"You'd rather ask in person?"

"Yeah, I think so…" Amelia wondered if she'd have the courage. She did seem to have more ability to be forward with Mel when they were alone.

"So when are you going to see her next?" Eliza asked. "Tonight?"

"No, she works until close tonight," said Amelia.

"And there's *no way* for you to see her after close?" Eliza asked, her tone almost taunting.

"I was planning on going to bed," Amelia said. "Like, soon actually."

"Are you going to be able to sleep with this on your mind?" It was almost as if Eliza was daring her to say yes, because she knew her better than that. She knew how Amelia's brain worked. And now that she'd said it out loud, there was no way Amelia was getting so much as a wink of sleep with this weighing on her mind.

"No," Amelia admitted.

"So are you going to go see her?" Eliza asked. "Go back to the bar without your *totally obnoxious* roommate?"

Amelia shook her head. "I couldn't ask her while she's working—even if I did go back alone." Amelia looked at her watch. It was already pretty late, but closing time was a while off yet. *Will this really keep me up?*

"See if you can hook up once she's off," Eliza said. It sounded more like a command than a suggestion.

"Yeah, okay." Amelia picked up her phone again. 'Want to meet up after work?' she texted.

'I wish I could, but I have some things I have to do,' Mel replied right away.

'What kind of things?' Amelia asked.

'We're still on for tomorrow right? Isn't it late for you to still be up?'

"Oooh, she didn't answer your question," Eliza said, her eyes widening, her expression far too excited.

Amelia felt her stomach drop. *Mel really is hiding something.* Amelia texted back, 'Yeah. I guess I should go to bed. What time tomorrow?'

'I'll want to get some sleep, but really any time is good. I have all day free and I'd love to spend it with you, beautiful,' Mel responded back.

"Smooth," Eliza rolled her eyes. "What do you say, *beautiful*?"

'Me too. Text me when you wake up and I'll head over,' Amelia responded.

'Will do. Sleep well, my dear.'

'You too.'

"Do you think you can really wait all night wondering? Knowing she has 'things' to do tonight and 'things' aren't *you*? I mean, if she's hiding something and she doesn't want you to know what she's doing after work..." Eliza raised her eyebrows at Amelia.

"I'm going to try." Amelia stood. "Goodnight."

"See you soon," Eliza replied with a knowing smile.

Amelia went to bed filled with a deep sense of sadness and fear that her worst suspicions could come true. *What if the thing she's doing tonight after work is the thing she's hiding?* She couldn't stop thinking the same thought over and over. Amelia tossed and turned but didn't fall asleep. She looked at the clock. It was after one-thirty in the morning. Amelia gave in to her fear and climbed out of bed. Eliza was still sitting in the living room, right where she'd left her.

"Okay, fine. You win. I can't sleep," Amelia admitted. "I want to know what she's doing tonight."

"I knew it!" Eliza popped up off the sofa. "Now hurry up; slip into something black and sexy—minus the sexy—and let's go play Nancy Drew."

Amelia knew she shouldn't do as Eliza suggested. She knew that spying on her girlfriend wasn't the healthy thing to do. *If I get caught, I could ruin everything.* And yet that nagging suspicion deep in her gut was pushing her, telling her that Eliza was right and that she had to do this.

Amelia went to her room. She dug out her one pair of black slacks and a black t-shirt. When she came back out, she found Eliza dressed in yoga pants and a black hoodie.

"This is ridiculous," Amelia said, looking at the two of them—dressed like wanna-be cat burglars. "We're dressed like TV characters."

"How many times have we been watching TV and you've actually yelled at the characters for trying to be stealthy in bright colors?" Eliza asked as she pulled her blonde hair into a ponytail.

"Like, maybe once?" Amelia shrugged.

"More than once," Eliza insisted, grabbing Amelia by the hand. "Now shut up and let's get going before we miss our chance."

It was a quarter 'til two; at this point they'd have to drive to be sure to make it to North River before Mel left. Amelia let herself be led outside to Eliza's car. Beyond the yellow glow of the streetlamp, the night was as dark as pitch with no moon visible in the sky.

"My mind misgives some consequence yet hanging in the stars," Amelia whispered to herself as she closed the car door.

"Nice one. Now buckle in; let's go." Eliza threw the car into drive and they darted off down the street toward North River.

Eliza arrived at the end of the alleyway that ran behind and parked across the street, under a tree—away from the one light at the end of the lane. From here they could just make out the back door of North River where Mel would exit after she'd locked up for the night.

"I have a bad feeling about this," Amelia muttered.

"That's why we're here." Eliza squinted in the direction of the alley. "We should have brought binoculars," she said. "How long do you think it'll take for her to come out?"

"I don't know. She's probably in the process of closing right now, but that could take some time…" Amelia leaned her head back and closed her eyes. "Ugh, this is a terrible idea. We shouldn't have come."

"Nonsense, it's a fine idea…" Eliza looked around the car. "Although we also should have brought snacks. What's a stakeout without snacks? We are rubbish detectives."

They waited for what felt like an eternity. Amelia was just starting to nod off when Eliza nudged her with her elbow.

"But soft," Eliza whispered. "What light through yonder *door* breaks."

Amelia looked up. Down the alley, she could just make out Mel's form, stepping out from the glow of the doorway into the dark night. Mel walked down the alley toward the street, coming closer and closer to where they sat in their car. Mel's head kept turning left to right and back, looking for something. Or someone.

What if she catches us? Amelia's heart hammered in her ears. But Mel didn't move any closer. She waited at the corner where the alley met the street. The light affixed to the wall of the building behind her cast long shadows, making Mel a dark silhouette—her face hidden and unreadable.

"What's she doing?" Eliza asked in a whisper.

"Nothing."

"Well I can see that she's doing nothing, but *why* is she doing nothing? Shouldn't she—" Eliza stopped when a small black car pulled up to the corner. Mel stepped toward the car but didn't reach for the door.

"She's talking to the driver. Can you tell what they're saying?" Amelia asked.

"I can get you a monkey that's weak but I have two parrots," Eliza said with a laugh. "Yeah, I can't read lips."

"Shut up, somebody's getting out of the car."

A man climbed out of the vehicle and moved towards Mel. Her hands were up as she backed slowly away from the advancing man. She was saying something. The man was shouting back. Amelia could almost hear him. She rolled the window down a crack.

"—late and short!"

"I'll make it up I just…" Mel's voice was muffled and hard to understand.

"You always say that like you think you can just get away with it," the man growled, advancing on Mel. She put her hands up over her face and he punched her in the stomach.

"Mel!" Amelia reached for the door, but Eliza held her back.

"Don't! It's not safe."

"But—" Amelia watched with horror as the man punched Mel a second time, this time on the side of her head. Mel stumbled; the man shoved her down and kicked her.

Amelia wrenched out of Eliza's grip and jumped out of the car. "Mel!" she shouted. The man turned away from Mel, and Amelia froze. She couldn't see his face but she knew he could see hers. What would he do? He seemed to consider his options for a moment.

"Do better, or it gets worse," the man said over his shoulder to Mel, before he got in his car and sped off. Amelia rushed to Mel's side.

"Oh my God. Are you okay?"

"What are you doing here?" Mel groaned as she slowly sat up. Her head was bleeding—it must have hit the pavement—and she was clearly in pain.

"Something felt off, I just had this feeling—"

"Is she okay?" Eliza was jogging across the street.

"I'm fine." Mel winced. "I just need to catch my breath."

The way she was holding her side made Amelia think she might have broken ribs. "Let me take you to the hospital."

"No," Mel said firmly.

"But you're hurt!"

"I can't afford it, okay!" Mel snapped and Amelia fell silent. She helped Mel to her feet.

"At least let us take you back to your apartment," Eliza insisted.

Slowly Mel nodded. "Yeah, okay. Thanks." She let Amelia lead her to the car. She grimaced as she sat down in the passenger seat. It was hard to see Mel in so much pain.

If I'd gotten out of the car sooner... Amelia felt guilty, but at the same time she was grateful that she'd been there at all.

"Who was that guy?" Eliza asked as they drove.

"None of your business," Mel said with a groan.

"He could have killed you!" Eliza protested.

"Yeah, and it *still* wouldn't be any of your fucking business," Mel grunted.

Eliza huffed but she didn't press it any further. When they arrived at Mel's building, Amelia jumped out of the car to help her.

"You don't have to help me; thanks for the ride, but I'm fine," Mel said when Amelia didn't get back in the car.

"Let me look after you tonight. Please," Amelia asked. Mel looked like she was going to argue, but after a beat she nodded. Amelia turned to stick her head in the car. "I'm staying with Mel."

"Of course you are." Eliza smiled and shook her head. "I'll see you when you get home."

"Thanks, Eliza." Amelia closed the door and Eliza drove off. She turned to Mel. "Let's get you to bed."

Chapter 13: Mel

Mel let Amelia help her shower; Amelia got her painkillers and an ice pack before they both laid down in bed. Mel didn't say much, and Amelia didn't push, for which Mel was grateful. She was still in shock over all that had transpired—Brad's escalated violence, and Amelia's sudden appearance with her roommate.

Ever since the adrenaline of the moment had worn off, Mel's whole body had been aching painfully. It hurt to breathe; she didn't know how she'd possibly be able to sleep. But once she was in bed, she found that the pull of exhaustion was stronger than the pain, and she fell asleep almost the instant her head hit the pillow.

The next morning Mel woke up before Amelia. She winced as she slipped out of bed and tiptoed to the bathroom. In the light of early morning, the events of last night felt like a dream. However the pain in her ribs reminded her that it was all too real. Mel looked at herself in the mirror. One side of her face was swollen—

her eye ringed with black. And on her forehead was an angry red patch of skin where her head had hit the ground. "I look like hell," Mel muttered to herself. She took out the elastic holding her hair and let it fall forward into her face. Her hair didn't really *hide* her injuries, but it did obscure them somewhat. She hoped that Amelia wouldn't over-react and try to take her to the hospital again.

Just show her you're doing alright, Mel thought. If she could make Amelia breakfast, maybe that would serve as proof that she was fine and didn't need more help.

Mel put her hand over her aching ribs as she moved about the kitchen. The pressure helped. *Maybe I can wrap it with something.* Mel winced and sucked in air between her teeth as she bent to retrieve her frying pan. She wished she could afford a trip to urgent care. She could use something a little stronger than Tylenol.

Mel pulled out her ingredients and got to work chopping vegetables. Cooking helped take her mind off the pain. Mel was just about done making breakfast when Amelia stumbled out of bed, rubbing sleep from her eyes.

"How are you feeling?" Amelia asked, looking her over.

Mel had been holding her side, but under Amelia's gaze she dropped her hand and smiled. "Good morning, beautiful."

"How are you feeling?" Amelia repeated.

"I'm okay," Mel began. Amelia gave her a stern look. "I've been better," she amended. "But I've also been worse, so I know I'll be fine. Don't worry."

Amelia stepped up to Mel and put a hand gingerly on the uninjured side of her face. "I'm going to worry, because I love you. That's part of what love is—caring about what happens to you."

"Thanks. I love you too." Mel put her hand over Amelia's and held it against her cheek. "I guess I'm just not used to having somebody who cares." She dropped her hand. "Now sit down, I'm making you breakfast."

"You don't have to do that," Amelia said.

"I wanted to," Mel insisted. She noticed Amelia eyeing the pan of bacon sitting on the stovetop and laughed. "Don't worry, I know the bacon would probably make you sick. That's for me." She winked. "Now sit down and let me feed you, gorgeous."

Smiling sheepishly, Amelia sat, and Mel followed with a plate in each hand. Bacon and eggs for herself, and for Amelia, something a bit lighter.

"For you, a veggie omelet." Mel set the plate in front of Amelia.

"It looks really good," Amelia said, although her expression wasn't entirely convincing.

"I don't expect you to necessarily love it, but it shouldn't make you sick." Mel smiled at her. "I'd like you to try it, but you don't have to eat it if you don't want to."

"Thank you, really. I honestly haven't had an omelet in a long time; I, uh, I don't normally eat breakfast at all…" Amelia took one bite, and then another. "It's good," she said, nodding.

"I'm glad."

"So, are you going to tell me the whole story?" Amelia asked as she ate. "About last night?"

Mel took a bite of bacon and nodded. "Yeah. I guess I owe you the whole truth. If I love you, I should trust you with that. But just promise me something."

"What?"

"That you won't tell anybody and won't try to help." Mel didn't want Amelia to get mixed up in the situation.

And above everything she didn't want Amelia to end up getting hurt. "I got myself into this mess and I'll get myself out, but it's embarrassing." Mel looked earnestly at her and Amelia nodded.

"I promise."

"Okay, so you know how I told you that I moved here because of my ex-girlfriend? And that she wasn't exactly who she said she was?" Mel asked.

"Yeah."

"Well, when I moved here, she told me she needed a new place and that she needed my help. She said she had this vindictive ex and that he was stalking her and trying to ruin her life."

"Wait, he?" Amelia interrupted.

"She's bisexual; her ex was a man. But she swore that she loved me and wanted to build a life with me. But she claimed she couldn't set anything up in her name, because of him. So when we found an apartment, I put it under my name. I didn't have any money, but she had cash. So I put the cash in my bank account and signed the lease. I should have figured something was fishy. We'd only just met, and she got me to sign a lease while I was totally financially dependent on her. I'm so stupid." Mel found she couldn't look Amelia in the eye while she told the tale. It was too mortifying. But Amelia reached out and squeezed her hand.

"You're not stupid; you were tricked," she said. "What happened to her?"

Mel let out a deep sigh. "Well, it turned out that her ex-boyfriend was actually her current *husband*. One day I got home he was there with her, in our bed."

"Oh shit."

"Yeah." Mel ground her teeth. She didn't like thinking about that day. "They were both so high off their faces that they didn't even bother to stop fucking when I showed up."

"What did you do?" Amelia asked.

"I kicked her out. I told her she could come back for her stuff, but apparently, I should have been more specific about how she should go about that," Mel said bitterly.

"What do you mean?"

When Mel described what Brad and Heidi had done to the apartment and all her things, Amelia gaped at her. And when she explained how the landlord was still holding her responsible, Amelia looked like she might fall over from the shock of it all.

"That… that sucks," she said.

"Yeah well, if that was the end of the story it would be one thing. I'd still be pretty broke, but I wouldn't be…" Mel gestured to her face. "You know, broken."

Amelia looked at her expectantly and Mel let out another heavy sigh. "You know, I was making progress. It was slow but I had a plan… But then my ex's husband showed up and started demanding their money back on pain of… pain, should I refuse." Mel let out a bitter laugh. "I'm doing my best but clearly he doesn't think that's quite good enough." Again she gestured to her face.

"Oh my God, that's horrible." Amelia was looking at her with such pity.

Mel gave her a lop-sided smile. "I'm getting close though—one more month and I should be square. Then I can focus on my credit card debt like a normal person. The interest might be a bitch, but at least MasterCard isn't going to punch me." She laughed ruefully.

Amelia stared, dumbfounded.

"You know, if this is too much… if you don't want to keep seeing me—" Mel began.

"Of course it doesn't make me not want to see you!" Amelia cut in. She squeezed Mel's hand again. "It makes me want to help you."

Mel shook her head. "There's nothing you can do to help."

"But there has to be," Amelia insisted. "I have some savings—"

"No!" Mel snapped. It came out so loud and sharp that Amelia sat back.

"I'm only offering—"

"This is why I didn't want to tell you." Mel shook her head and looked seriously at Amelia. "I want to be your girlfriend, not your charity case. I don't want anything to change between us."

"Okay, but—"

"No, no buts. It's embarrassing enough as it is. I can take care of it. I *will* take care of it. But I need to do it on my own," Mel insisted stubbornly.

"Fine, but if I am your girlfriend, I get to care about your wellbeing. That's part of what a relationship is. So maybe you won't take my help dealing with the situation directly, but at least let me be here to support you emotionally." Amelia stood and, taking Mel's hand, and gently pulled her out of her chair. "*A friend is someone who helps you up when you are down and if they can't, they lay down beside you and listen.*' And a girlfriend is just extra good at the laying down with you part."

Amelia winked, and Mel laughed out loud, then winced as pain stabbed through her chest.

"That's not Shakespeare," she said.

"No, it's Winnie the Pooh." Amelia smiled and looked into Mel's eyes. "I mean it though. I'm here to pick you up when you fall down. But you have to be willing to let me know when you fall."

"I will," Mel promised.

"Thank you." Amelia kissed her lightly on the lips.

"Thank you," Mel parroted, kissing her back. "Just please, promise me you won't tell anybody else."

"What about Eliza?" Amelia asked. "She saw him hit you. What should I tell her?"

Mel groaned. "Shit. I forgot about that." Eliza seemed to have a special talent for being in the wrong place at the wrong time. Not that there was a right place or time, since if Mel had her way Eliza wouldn't be anywhere near her ever.

"She's going to pester me until I tell her *something*," Amelia warned. "There's no way that Eliza will just let something like this go, no questions asked."

"Can't you just tell her to mind her own business?" Mel asked.

"I can, but she won't."

Mel sighed. "Fine. Tell her I still have some beef with an old friend. She doesn't need details. Tell her it's over. There's nothing for her to worry about."

"Okay," Amelia agreed.

"Promise?" Mel asked.

"I promise," Amelia agreed.

Mel could feel herself relax. It was over, she'd told Amelia, and Amelia was still there. Nothing had to change between them. And in a month, her debt would be paid, and she would be done with Brad and Heidi forever. Bruised ribs aside, life was starting to look up.

Chapter 14: Amelia

As expected, Eliza was *eagerly* anticipating an update when Amelia returned home. She was sitting in the living room, reading and listening to soft music. She immediately put down her book when Amelia entered the room.

"You've been *far* too quiet on text this weekend," Eliza scolded.

"Sorry, I was a bit preoccupied. I wanted to give Mel my full attention." Amelia tried to sound casual. She wasn't sure exactly what she was going to tell Eliza. Her 'bestie' had a remarkable talent for sensing if she wasn't being completely honest about something.

"So…?" Eliza looked at her expectantly, her voice raised in question.

"So what?" Amelia feigned confusion.

Eliza tilted her head and gave Amelia a stern look. "You know exactly what, Amelia Bedelia." She stared at Amelia. Amelia stared back. She still had no idea what to say; stalling seemed like her best option. With an exasperated sigh, Eliza stood up. She took Amelia by the hand and dragged her to the couch. "Come here, sit down, and spill it," she said.

"It's not really my story to tell," Amelia protested.

"Oh, whatever! She knows I saw what happened. It's not like I don't know something's up." Eliza rolled her eyes to the ceiling.

"Sure but—"

"But nothing," Eliza interrupted. "You have to tell me. You told me your theories, didn't you?"

"So?" Amelia didn't see what bearing that had on anything. But evidently, it was clear to Eliza because she rolled her eyes again and made one of her 'how are you so stupid' faces.

"So, unless you tell me otherwise that's all I have to go on! I'll just assume you were right all along."

Amelia wrinkled her nose.

"Come on," Eliza coaxed. "Is it really an ex-boyfriend or spurned secret lover? Is Mel secretly bi? Was she cheating?" Eliza wiggled her eyebrows suggestively.

"No, she was never cheating." Amelia shook her head. "It's nothing like that, okay?"

"So why is she having a *secret rendezvous* with a man? Who was that guy?"

Amelia didn't like the insinuation Eliza was making with the phrase 'secret rendezvous.' Especially given that the truth was far less titillating. "He's her ex-girlfriend's husband," Amelia said flatly. "She was never involved with him, okay?"

"So her ex-girlfriend is the cheating bisexual?" Eliza asked, sounding far too excited by the idea.

"What? I mean, I guess Mel was still seeing her when—" Amelia began before catching herself. "Hey, cut it out. I shouldn't be talking about this. And anyway, you shouldn't say stuff like that, you know. It's a terrible stereotype that bi people are cheaters."

Eliza waved her hand in a dismissive gesture. "Oh save your speech, Amelia. I don't think all bi people are cheaters and you know it. You're trying to change the subject."

"No, I'm not," Amelia lied. She stood up from the sofa and walked away from Eliza toward the kitchen. She'd eaten a huge breakfast at Mel's but somehow she was already hungry again. She looked at her watch. It was already after four. *How did it get that late?*

"Well, so what did he want?" Eliza asked, following her to the kitchen.

"None of your business," Amelia said. "Do you want dinner? I'm going to make some pasta."

"Sure," Eliza agreed. "And I'll pour us each a glass of wine."

"Why?"

"You have to have wine with pasta, it's basically a rule," Eliza said as she poured two large glasses. "Besides, you need to loosen up. This whole drama with your girl clearly has you stressed."

Amelia accepted the wine, although it wasn't Mel who was stressing her out, it was Eliza. She and Mel had had a lovely time together today—injuries and dramatic revelations aside. "I'm not stressed. I was, but it's okay. Mel's—"

"Oh! How is Mel feeling today? Was she hurt badly?" Eliza sighed. "Sorry, I'm a jerk for not asking that first. That is what's important, after all."

"She's okay," Amelia said. She sipped her wine as she waited for the pasta water to boil. "She's a little banged up but she's moving around well. She made me breakfast."

"That's good to hear," Eliza said sweetly. "It looked so painful last night."

"Yeah, I was worried," Amelia agreed. "If it were me, I probably would have gone to the hospital but she's really tough."

"She does seem like one tough lady," Eliza agreed. "Why would her ex-girlfriend's husband want to beat her up anyway? It doesn't even make sense. They've been broken up for a while, right? Why would he even bother still coming after her?"

"She owes them money," Amelia answered without thinking.

"Oh shit," Eliza said, and Amelia kicked herself for letting it slip. Eliza gestured vaguely with her wine glass. "I just assumed it was, like, jealousy or something. Like, continued payback for sleeping with his woman."

Amelia winced. That would have been a simpler explanation; she wished she'd thought of it before mentioning the money.

"So why does she owe them money?" Eliza asked.

Amelia shrugged. She'd already said too much. If Mel found out she would be upset; Amelia didn't want to dig that hole any deeper.

"Don't try to hold out on me, Amelia," Eliza tisked. "I'll get it out of you. You know you can't keep secrets from me." She laughed and Amelia felt her cheeks burn with the heat of embarrassment and wine. She knew Eliza was right. *Why can't I keep secrets from her?* It was like her roommate had a truth spell cast on her. *Or a truth serum*, Amelia thought looking at the near-empty wine glass in her hand. She set it down and turned to put the pasta in the water.

"Come on, what's the deal with the money?" Eliza asked again.

"Does it even matter?" Amelia said, not turning back. "I shouldn't have even told you that much, so could you drop it?"

Eliza put her arms around Amelia's shoulders from behind and squeezed. "Come on, bestie, I'm just curious. And maybe I could help."

"How could you help?" Amelia asked, wriggling free from Eliza's embrace.

"I have connections. Extortion is illegal, you know. If that's what he's doing."

Amelia considered. "I don't think it counts as extortion. It's just that her ex had given her money for rent and now they want it back."

"Is she still living in the same place as when she was with her ex?"

"No, that place got trashed."

"So why didn't she just give the money back? Did she spend it?" Eliza narrowed her eyes. "She doesn't, like, have a gambling problem or something, does she?"

"What? No!" Amelia protested. "But she has to pay rent through the end of the contract since it's her name on the lease. So he wants the money and the landlord wants the money. She didn't do anything wrong, she's just in a crappy situation." Amelia realized she was sharing too much again and clamped her mouth shut. *What is wrong with me?* Somehow defending Mel had turned into airing her dirty laundry. "Can we stop talking about this now?"

"But if we stop talking about it, I won't be able to help, and I'm starting to suspect that Mel could *really* use my help," Eliza said.

"Do you really think you could help?" Amelia asked, unsure.

"Absolutely. It's total crap that she'd be paying rent on a trashed apartment and still be on the hook to pay that money back to the dickholes who trashed it in the first place." Eliza shook her head, her blonde hair swooshing about her face. Her cheeks were pink, flushed from the wine, but she looked sincere. "I mean it, Amelia. I can help, but I'll need to talk to Mel."

Panic began to rise in Amelia's chest. "No, please. Then she'll know I told you. She'd be so upset with me! Please don't," Amelia begged.

Eliza put her hands on Amelia's shoulders and looked seriously into her friend's face. "If you love her, you should help her. And if she really loves you, she'll understand you were only trying to help by coming to me with this. It's good that you told me. Now come on, serve that pasta and give me the deets. We'll solve this and you will be her knight in shining armor."

Amelia really hoped Eliza was right. *If Eliza can help her, Mel will understand. Won't she?* It made sense, but at the same time, that didn't ease the knot in her chest. *Oh, God, I hope Mel doesn't hate me for this.*

Chapter 15: Mel

It had been a few days since Mel had told Amelia her whole shameful tale, but aside from being concerned about her healing wounds, Amelia hadn't said a thing about it, for which Mel was grateful. And she was ready to show that gratitude tonight. In bed.

Mel smiled to herself and rubbed her side. Although her ribcage was still a bit tender, there had been noticeable improvement over the last few days and Mel was eager to have sex again. She was really looking forward to telling Amelia as much.

When Amelia stepped through the door to North River during her midday shift, Mel grinned broadly. But her smile faded when Amelia was followed through the door by Eliza. *You love Amelia and she's Amelia's best friend,* she told herself. *You're not going to be able to avoid her entirely forever.*

"Hey, beautiful," Mel greeted Amelia with a smile as she sat down on her usual barstool. She leaned forward for a quick peck on the lips.

"Hey, how are you feeling?" Amelia asked.

"Pretty good," Mel replied. "See?" She moved her arms and stretched her torso to demonstrate how well she was healing. She wanted to add something suggestive, but Eliza hopped up on the stool beside Amelia and Mel swallowed her words.

"Hello, Mel," Eliza chirped brightly. "You're looking *good*," she purred, her eyes wandering over her in a way that made Mel uncomfortable. Eliza flashed her a lurid smile. "I think the bruises actually add to your tough girl image. Very sexy."

"Um, thanks, I guess?" Mel replied.

"I'm serious," Eliza continued, licking her plump pink lips and continuing to look at Mel in a blatantly objectifying manner. "Maybe I'm just horny from being so incredibly single, but you look delicious," Eliza said. She turned to Amelia. "Your girlfriend really is a total snack."

"Shut up, Eliza," Amelia said mildly.

"What can I get you ladies to drink?" Mel asked, trying to shift the spotlight off her looks.

"Nothing for me, thanks," Eliza said, setting a folder down in front of herself. "This is a working lunch." She opened the folder and clicked on her pen.

"So, Mel, I have a few questions. Let's start with the landlord. I'm going to need his contact information as well as details on the length of the lease and total amount owed."

Mel blinked at her. "What the fuck?" She looked from Eliza to Amelia and back.

"I'm here to help, clearly," Eliza said in a patronizing tone. "But I'm going to need more information in order to—"

"Stop." Mel slapped her hand down on the bar. "I didn't ask for your help. I didn't even want you to know—"

"Yes, yes, I know. But that's just stupid."

"Excuse me?" Mel fumed.

Eliza rolled her eyes and scoffed. "You're throwing away money you can't afford to throw away; you're probably spending thousands more than you have, and for no good reason. So set aside your ego and let me help you."

Mel stared at her, feeling the burn of anger and embarrassment. She didn't know how to deal with this.

She didn't want to deal with this. Not here, and certainly not with Eliza.

"Shove your 'help' up your ass, Eliza. This is none of your damn business," Mel growled.

"Don't be an idiot—"

"I'm not an idiot!" Mel snapped. "And I don't— I can't— Argh!" She tore off her apron and threw it down. "I'm done."

Anger was overwhelming her senses; she needed some space and time to herself to calm down. Mel shot Amelia a dark look before turning and walking through the back and out of the bar.

"Mel, wait!" Amelia called after her. To Mel's great annoyance, Amelia followed her through the kitchen and out the back door.

"Mel, I'm sorry," she said.

Mel stared at her, incredulous. "You're sorry? You're sorry?! You didn't seem to even realize you had something to be sorry for five minutes ago! I mean come on! You brought Eliza to my bar. Without warning. Knowing she was going to drag up all this— God! I can't believe you *told* her!" Mel was fuming. "You promised me!"

Tears glistened in Amelia's eyes and Mel had to turn away. Amelia grabbed her arm. "I really am sorry, Mel. And I didn't tell her everything, I swear. I just thought—"

"No, you didn't think," Mel snapped, pulling her arm away. "Because if you had thought, you would have remembered that I explicitly told you not to fucking tell anybody! And especially not your pain in the ass roommate!"

"But she might be able to help—"

"I told you I don't need help! Not yours and *certainly* not hers!"

"But she works in a law office and—"

"That's beside the point!" Mel shouted. "Goddamn it, Amelia! I loved you and I trusted you. And you betrayed that trust."

"I'm so sorry—"

"Just stop. Get out of my face. Get out of my bar. I don't want to see you or talk to you right now."

Amelia hesitated, her green eyes shining with tears. "I'm sorry," she whispered. "I love you, Mel. I never meant… I didn't think… I'm so sorry."

"Leave," Mel growled through gritted teeth. It was painful to see the tears that were now trickling down her girlfriend's cheeks, but the pain of betrayal burned hotter. She clenched her jaw to keep from screaming or crying as she watched Amelia slowly turn and walk back through the door into North River.

By the time Mel had composed herself and made her way back to the restaurant floor, Amelia and Eliza were gone. Mel was both relieved and incredibly sad. Part of her wanted so badly to just forgive Amelia and move on as if none of this had ever happened.

I can't just ignore this. If she betrayed me once, she could do it again, Mel told herself. She didn't know if she could survive another betrayal. The scars from Heidi were still too fresh. *I should never have started dating again. I should never have let myself fall in love.*

Chapter 16: Amelia

Amelia cried silently for the whole walk home. Eliza walked beside her, going on and on about how unfair Mel's reaction had been. Amelia felt like a total moron. She knew Mel didn't want her telling Eliza and yet somehow, she had not only told Eliza but let her get involved. *I should never have let Eliza ambush her like that*, Amelia chastised herself. She realized too late that she should have admitted her mistake to Mel right away. If she had done that and had brought Eliza's questions and suggestions to Mel herself, maybe Mel would have forgiven her and even taken the help. *I can't undo what I did.*

"You did the right thing telling me, you know," Eliza said. "Mel might not see that now but once I work my magic, she'll have no choice but to admit that you were right."

"Could you just drop it?" Amelia begged her roommate and supposed best friend as they let themselves into the house.

"No, I will not drop it," Eliza said, pursing her lips. "She's being ridiculous. I can help and I'll prove it. If she's too proud to accept the solutions I can arrange for her, well, then she's too stupid for you and you're better off without her anyway."

"She's not stupid," Amelia grumbled. As angry as she was at herself for betraying Mel, she was starting to get even angrier with Eliza and her persistent know-it-all attitude.

"*She* that is so yoked by a fool, methinks, should not be chronicled for wise," Eliza intoned.

"And she's not a fool."

"No dumb-dumb, I'm saying Heidi— You know, whatever. My point is she's not *smart*. If she were she wouldn't be in this situation—"

"It's not her fault!" Amelia snapped.

"Even if that's true, not accepting help is a choice she's making and it's a stupid one. Lucky for her I like challenging people's stupidity. It might take a bit longer without her cooperation, but—"

"Shut up, Eliza!" Amelia shouted, unable to stand it any longer. "Do whatever you want but just leave me out of it." Amelia stormed off to her room, but Eliza followed.

"I'm only doing this for you because you're my bestie, you know. I care about you."

"Yeah, well you have a funny way of showing it sometimes." Amelia slammed her door shut.

Eliza opened it. "Why are you so bent out of shape?" she asked.

I can't stay here, Amelia thought. She needed some time to herself to think and she wasn't going to get that if she stuck around the house. She needed space away from Eliza. It was the only way she was going to be able to figure out how to make things right with Mel. *If I keep listening to Eliza, I'll just make things worse.*

Amelia grabbed her suitcase from the closet and began to stuff it with clothing.

"What are you doing?" Eliza asked, eyes wide.

"I'm going to my sister's house for a day or two."

"What? Why?"

Amelia didn't look at Eliza as she continued to pack. "I need some time to clear my head, without you telling me what to think all the time."

"I do not tell you what to think, Amelia Bedelia, don't be dramatic."

Amelia zipped her suitcase shut. She pushed past Eliza and headed for the door. Eliza let her pass, a look of bored irritation on her pretty little face.

"Alright, fine," Eliza said, rolling her eyes. "You know, it sucks to be the smart level-headed one sometimes." She sighed. "Go have some sister time. 'Clear your head.' Whatever. The conclusion will be the same. In a few days you'll both be falling all over yourselves thanking me."

Amelia didn't dignify that with a response. She walked out the door without looking back.

~ ~ ~

Amelia's sister, Lynn, lived just outside of town in a new suburban housing development that abutted long cornfields. Amelia's nieces, who were at the very excitable ages of two and four years old, were thrilled when Aunt 'Melia showed up at their door unannounced. Lynn was very understanding. Amelia didn't fully explain the situation to her, but Lynn could be sympathetic without needing all the details.

During the thirty-minute ride to her sister's house, Amelia's head had started to clear. It didn't matter what

Eliza did or said, Amelia knew that she should not have shared things that weren't hers to share. Full stop. The only thing she could do now was to try and show Mel that she understood how wrong she had been and how truly remorseful she was. The only problem was that she had no idea how to do that. She'd sent her several apologetic texts but Mel hadn't responded.

Maybe she needs some time and space too, Amelia reasoned. While she waited to hear from Mel, she let herself get swept up playing with her nieces as her sister cooked dinner. Amelia joined the family for dinner. She managed to make it through the evening without breaking down, although the anxiety in her was building. She'd chatted with her sister over evening coffee, all the while keeping one eye on her phone, hoping desperately to hear from Mel.

When Lynn left her to put the kids to bed and she still hadn't heard from Mel, Amelia retreated to the guestroom. In the privacy and solitude of the familiar room, her fear of losing Mel seemed amplified. *I have to do something.*

She took out her laptop. Sitting on the bed, Amelia wrote a three-page apology letter. When she read it over, she realized it was basically a formal essay on contrition. She deleted it and tried again. Her second attempt was somehow even longer and made almost no sense. The written word was failing her and she didn't know how else to cope. The strong possibility that her relationship was over hit Amelia like a speeding train. She put away her laptop and sent Mel one last text.

'You gave me a do-over once. Can you bring yourself to give me a second chance again?'

Chapter 17: Mel

Mel left her phone in back and worked on autopilot all day—not wanting to think about Amelia or their fight. She took her time shutting down the bar. She let Mark have one more drink than she probably should have, but she stuck around to make sure he got in a cab. After he was gone, she did the morning prep work. She knew she was just avoiding her feelings, and she knew it couldn't last forever. Eventually Mel ran out of excuses to keep working. She said goodnight to North River and went home.

Alone in her apartment it was harder to keep thoughts of Amelia at bay. *I should at least check my texts.* Mel still hadn't so much as looked at her phone. She didn't have anything to say to Amelia and she didn't know what she wanted Amelia to say. So what was the point? Mel flopped down in bed and unlocked her phone. There were fewer texts than she was expecting but the last one made her think.

'You gave me a do-over once. Can you bring yourself to give me a second chance again?'

She had given Amelia a do-over before, when Amelia had all but ignored her on their first date. Mel thought about that night, months ago. At the time, Mel had taken Amelia's inattention to mean that she wasn't really interested in her. But in reality, Amelia had been preoccupied worrying about her roommate.

Fucking Eliza. Just the thought of that blonde bitch made Mel's anger flare again. *Who am I more angry with, Amelia or Eliza?* When she asked herself, she realized she honestly wasn't sure. Eliza was a raging cunt, and part of Mel really wanted to punch her in her smug little face. But she'd always disliked Eliza. She had *loved* Amelia—she still loved Amelia. But after what Amelia had done, Mel wasn't sure that love was enough.

~ ~ ~

Mel woke up the next morning feeling sore and crabby. She didn't even remember falling asleep. Mel looked out the window. "Oh good, gray and rainy, just like my mood. How fitting," she muttered to herself.

As she dressed for work, Mel realized she'd never texted Amelia back. She picked up her phone. There were no new messages. *Why would there be? She's probably been asleep this whole time.* She read Amelia's last text over again. *Can I give her another second chance?* After few minutes of hesitation Mel replied.

'I'll think about it.'

It was all she could say because it was all she could promise. Mel silenced her phone, stuffed it in her pocket, and went to work.

Every time the door to North River opened Mel looked up, half expecting to see Amelia walking through; not sure if she wanted her to or not. But Amelia never showed. Mark, however, was back on his customary barstool at his usual hour, just like clockwork.

"I wasn't sure I'd see you today, Mark," Mel said as she poured his beer. "We had a late night last night, you and I."

Mark waved a weather-worn hand at her. "Eh. A little thing like that isn't going to keep a regular drunk like me from doing what I do." He lifted his glass to her, and Mel laughed.

"Speaking of regulars, where's your pretty girlfriend, Melody?" Mark asked.

"Not sure I have a girlfriend anymore, Mark," Mel replied with casual indifference.

"Trouble in paradise?" Sebastian set his tray on the bar and gave Mel a questioning look.

"Yeah, we had a fight." Mel shrugged. She shot Mark a lopsided grin. "Chicks? Am I right?" she asked with a wink.

Mark laughed.

"Oh no! What happened?" Sebastian asked, looking overly concerned.

"Eh." Mel shrugged again. "I told her some personal shit and asked her not to share it and she went and blabbed it to her asinine roommate."

"That sucks," Sebastian said with far more sympathy than Mel was comfortable with.

"That's a shitty thing to do, sorry to hear it, Melody," Mark chimed in.

"She didn't do it to be a bitch or anything," Mel said, turning away from Sebastian and his big blue eyes with their oh-poor-you expression. "I mean, it was a shitty thing to do but she really just wants to '*help*.'" Mel rolled her eyes on the word 'help.'

"And you're mad at her for that?" Sebastian asked.

"I don't need help." Mel smiled at Mark. "Do I look like somebody who needs help?"

"I don't know, but I think you're the one being a chick," Mark responded with a snort.

"Oh what do you know?" Mel shook her head good naturedly. "Need another, Mark?"

She could tell Sebastian was staring at her as she poured Mark another beer. "What?" she asked, turning to him. "Don't you tell me I'm being a girl. He can get away with it, you can't."

Sebastian put up his hands. "I'm just saying, I seem to recall telling you to get help—"

"I don't need help," Mel said sharply, her calm let-it-slide, service industry demeanor starting to erode under his thoughtful gaze.

"Everybody needs help sometimes. It doesn't make you any less of a badass to admit that, Mel," Sebastian said. "In fact, I think sometimes it takes a lot more strength to ask for help when you need it."

"What are you, a walking fortune cookie?" She shrugged Sebastian off, but his words stuck with her. Mel didn't want to admit that he may have a point—that they both did. *I am being kind of a chick.* What she'd said earlier was true: Amelia hadn't spilled her secrets out of malice, but out of a misplaced desire to help. If Mel admitted that Amelia's attempt to help *wasn't* misplaced, then she also needed to admit that Amelia might deserve to be forgiven.

It was one mistake. Can't I forgive one mistake? Amelia had been very forgiving when the truth of Mel's past had come out. She'd been nothing but understanding. *I hid things from her, and she found out the hard way. She could have easily chosen to leave me right then, but she didn't.* Amelia hadn't left; she had only wanted to help. And even if she'd gone about that the wrong way, Mel couldn't ignore the good intention behind it.

The more she thought about it, the more Mel knew she needed to talk to Amelia. She still loved her and she knew she needed to forgive her. And, as hard as it would be, she also would have to admit that she needed help. *I have to swallow my pride and do the right thing here for both of us.* Once Mel had made peace with that decision, she couldn't wait. She traded shifts with Sebastian and left North River at eight—as soon the dinner crowd had cleared.

Amelia had said she was waiting to be forgiven, so what better way than to go to her and clear everything up in person?

Mel took off on foot, headed for Amelia's house. It was drizzling when she left North River, but by the time she reached Amelia's block it was pouring down in sheets.

Mel ran the last few yards until she was at Amelia's door. She huddled close to the house to avoid the deluge and knocked on the door. Through the window, Mel could see light and shadows moving inside. She was both anxious and relieved, knowing that soon this fight between her and Amelia would be over.

However, when the door opened, it wasn't Amelia who drew her inside, it was Eliza.

"Oh my God! You're soaked!" Eliza exclaimed, pulling Mel inside and closing the door behind her before Mel had the chance to say a word. "Jesus, Mel, you look like a drowned rat!"

"Thanks, you're so sweet," Mel said sourly. She didn't want to deal with Eliza. In her haste to see Amelia, she'd honestly forgotten that Eliza might be there at all. She might have left if it weren't for the cold rain falling from the sky in buckets.

"Give me your coat," Eliza demanded. Although she didn't wait for Mel to react before peeling the soaking jacket from Mel's shivering body.

"Is Amelia home?" Mel managed through chattering teeth as Eliza wrestled away her outer layer.

Eliza shook her head. "Not at the moment." She draped Mel's coat over the radiator and then turned back to give her an appraising look. "You're still soaked through. Here, let me get you something dry to wear."

Mel tried to protest but Eliza was insistent.

"Do you know when Amelia will be back?" Mel asked as Eliza rummaged through an old overflowing dresser.

"Hard to say," Eliza replied. "She's with her sister. If they get in one of their 'sister chat' moods she can be there for ages… Here." Eliza thrust a t-shirt and sweatpants into Mel's arms.

"Maybe I should just come back," Mel said, inspecting the clothing with trepidation.

"Nonsense! You should totally stay! I'm sure she'll be home soon. Besides, the two of us have things to talk about."

"What do you mean?" Mel asked warily.

"I mean, despite your lack of cooperation I did some digging and I think you'll like what I found."

"Found what? What are you talking about?"

Eliza sighed and rolled her eyes like she was talking to a foolish child. "Found solutions to your little problems, obviously."

"But how—"

"Well, Amelia knew your ex's name was Heidi and her husband's name was Brad, so I checked public records. Her full name was Heidi Ruffalo, right?"

"How did you—"

"It's not hard if you know where to look. There aren't a lot of Brad and Heidi's out there, you know. Plus, the drug convictions made them easier to find."

"Drug convictions?" Mel was seriously confused.

"Yup." Eliza smirked. "Plus, like you said, your name was on the lease. So that wasn't exactly hard to find either."

"But why did you—"

"To help you, of course," Eliza said, interrupting her yet again. "After some seriously brilliant sleuthing on my part, I talked to my colleagues and we think we can solve your little stalker problem and at the very least get you out of that ridiculous lease."

"Really?" Mel asked, surprised and overwhelmed by all that Eliza was saying. "How?"

"Go change and I'll tell you all about it," Eliza said, giving Mel a little push in the direction of the bathroom.

Mel did as Eliza instructed. The cold rain had completely soaked through Mel's clothes and the chill was nearly bone deep; the warm, dry clothes felt comforting. When she was changed, she found Eliza waiting for her on the living room sofa.

Looking at her, Mel couldn't help but notice that Eliza wasn't wearing all that much herself—only a tiny tank top that showed off a fair amount of her bra-less chest and a pair of blue-striped pajama shorts so tiny that her ass peeked out from beneath them.

As much as she didn't like Eliza, looking at her there on the sofa, in the soft light of the one illuminated reading lamp, Mel could understand why Amelia might have had a crush on her. Eliza was pushy and obnoxious, but she was also quite attractive.

"Come, sit. Let me tell you all about my plans." Eliza beckoned her over and pressed a large glass of wine into her hand. Mel didn't normally drink wine, but she accepted the glass from Eliza and sat down. Despite her earlier trepidation, Mel found she was eager to hear more about Eliza's 'sleuthing' and her supposed plan.

"Okay, you've caught my interest," Mel admitted. "What did you figure out?"

Eliza explained the process in great detail—she was clearly proud of her detective work and of the legal maneuvering she and her colleagues had cooked up. It started out easy enough to follow. Heidi and Brad had been forced to split because he was incarcerated on several drug charges. It was around the time when he'd been arrested that Mel had started chatting with Heidi. There was a warrant out for Heidi as well, but she'd managed to evade arrest.

"So she wasn't hiding from Brad, she was hiding from the cops?" Mel was stunned.

"It looks that way," Eliza agreed. "Which is pretty handy information to have if you want to wriggle out from under her thumb."

"How am I going to do that? And what about the landlord?" Mel asked. She no longer cared who the information was coming from, it was information that could actually help.

Eliza continued to explain, moving from background on Heidi and Brad, to the landlord and housing laws, then finally to ways Mel could excise herself from both situations.

Mel had an increasingly difficult time tracking the details, partly because it was so steeped in technical terms she didn't understand, and partly because Eliza kept refilling her wine until her head was swimming in a drunken fog.

Mel may not have understood all that Eliza said, but Eliza's optimistic enthusiasm was catching. She went from forgiving to appreciative of the fact that Amelia had broken her promise and spilled her secrets. And she was starting to see Eliza in a new light—a hazy drunken light, but one that made her see Eliza as the kind, helpful, and beautiful roommate Amelia had sworn she could be.

"Maybe I misjudged you, Eliza," Mel said, her words slurring slightly. "Maybe you are a good friend." Mel patted Eliza's leg.

Eliza smiled wickedly. "I'm not *that* good of a friend," she said in a low voice. Without warning, she climbed on top of Mel, straddling her legs and sitting down into her lap until they were nose-to-nose. Mel sat, stunned as Eliza quickly pulled her tank top up and over her head, exposing her supple breasts and hard pink nipples barely two inches from Mel's face.

"What are you—" Mel began, but Eliza cut her off with a kiss. Mel's head was spinning like Dorothy Gale stuck in the twister. She felt like she was in a horribly confusing dream.

Eliza grabbed Mel's hands and placed them firmly on her back side. Eliza's ass was almost perfectly round; Mel instinctively squeezed her cheeks. Eliza moaned and pulled Mel's hands further beneath the fabric of her shorts until Mel's fingers found the edges of her slit. The wetness Mel felt there sent an involuntary shock of arousal through her body and she gasped.

Eliza kept one hand on Mel's—guiding it deeper— while her other hand came around to the back of Mel's head. Eliza's nails raked across Mel's scalp. She dug her fingers into Mel's hair and pulled hard. When Mel opened her mouth in another gasp, Eliza pushed that open mouth against her breast.

Mel felt Eliza's hard nipple against her tongue. Her head spun with wine and confusion; she began to lick and suck instinctually. Some part of Mel's brain knew this was wrong—that she shouldn't be doing any of this—but her mind was so deeply mired in wine and the onslaught of sensation that she couldn't get a hold of enough self-control to stop. Eliza began to move her hips, grinding against Mel's torso while fucking herself with Mel's fingers.

"Oh God, oh God," Eliza moaned. Her breathing came harder as her hips moved faster. She held Mel's head against her breast with an iron grip. Mel could hardly breathe, and yet she kept sucking, licking, and biting. She was entirely lost in the dizzying, confusing, and oh-so-very-wrong moment. When Eliza came, she threw her head back and screamed, her body convulsing atop Mel's.

"Fuck, I needed that," Eliza sighed, releasing her grip on Mel's hair and hand.

Mel was still confused and drunk, but after Eliza's performance, she was also flush with heat. But when she opened her eyes and looked up past Eliza's shoulder, all the warmth turned to ice. "Amelia."

Chapter 18: Amelia

Amelia's heart stopped when she walked into her house to find her best friend astride her girlfriend, riding her. She was too stunned for words. She stood motionless watching as Eliza bucked against Mel, Mel's face pressed against her breast. When Eliza came, the sound of her pleasure-filled scream turned Amelia's stomach. She felt like she might be sick. Her eyes filled with tears.

That's when Mel saw her. "Amelia."

Still, Amelia stood frozen—her body starting to shake.

Eliza turned her head and looked at her. She *smiled*. "Oops," she said, with no remorse in her voice as she hopped off of Mel's lap.

"What are you… what were you… how could you?" Amelia asked, stumbling over her words as tears began to trickle from her eyes.

Mel scrambled to her feet. "I'm sorry, I didn't—" she began.

"Oh calm down," Eliza interrupted. She grabbed her shirt from the sofa and pulled it on, her motions casual; her expression indifferent. "Mel was just so grateful for all the help I can give her. And you know I've been in a bit of a dry spell," she said by way of explanation.

Hearing her say Mel's name made something inside Amelia snap. "She's *my* girlfriend, Eliza!" she screeched.

"I thought you were on a break." Eliza tittered.

"Like hell!" Amelia shot back.

Mel began to stumble forward towards her, her motions looking awkward and unbalanced. Amelia noticed the wine glasses and bottles. *She's drunk,* Amelia thought. She looked at Eliza. She didn't seem at all affected. *She got Mel drunk on purpose*, Amelia realized.

"I didn't mean to. I don't know what happened," Mel said, her words slurring. "I am so, so sorry."

"Get out," Amelia growled.

Mel hung her head and began to gather her things.

"Not you, Mel," Amelia amended, her voice quivering. "Eliza. You need to leave."

"Excuse me?" Eliza looked stunned—Mel doubly so.

"You heard me," Amelia said, trying hard to keep her voice steady. She was ready to start bawling—she could feel the burn at the back of her throat—but she needed Eliza gone before that happened.

Eliza rolled her eyes and shook her head. "This is *my* house, Amelia Bedelia. I'm not going anywhere. I'm sorry if I upset you, but it was just a little sex. Hell, it was *barely* sex. You'll get over it and live happily ever after with your bar chick. Don't overreact."

"Overreact?" Amelia squeaked. "What… how… how do you expect me to react?"

"Honestly, I expect you to overreact," Eliza said, sounding almost bored. "It's what you do."

"Jesus Christ, what is wrong with you?" Mel said suddenly. Amelia looked at her. She was glaring at Eliza. "Could you stop being a total bitch for like five seconds and leave us alone?"

"Fine," Eliza acquiesced with a sigh. "I'll be in my room if you need me." She turned on her heel and walked off, head held high as if she'd done no wrong.

"Thank you," Amelia said.

"Amelia, I am so, so sorry," Mel began when Eliza was out of the room.

Amelia squeezed her eyes shut, fighting tears. But when she closed her eyes all she could see was her best friend cumming atop her girlfriend. "I can't…" She shook her head. She looked at Mel. "How? How could you?"

Mel took her hand. "I'm sorry. I don't even know what happened. One second we were talking and the next—"

"But why were you even talking?" Amelia asked, wrenching her hand from Mel's. "How did you end up with her at all? You hate her!"

"I was waiting for you," Mel said, sounding drunk and stupid.

"Waiting? I was at my sister's!" Hurt and confusion were morphing into anger as Amelia spoke. She glared at Mel. "I didn't know you'd be here! Why would you come here?"

"I came here looking for you," Mel insisted.

"But I wasn't here!" Amelia screeched. "What if I hadn't come home? Oh my God, Mel. You… you just… with Eliza!" She couldn't even bring herself to say the words. There was a lump in her throat and she knew she was about to cry. "I just don't understand. How could you be waiting for me when I didn't even know you were here?"

"You said you'd be *here* if I wanted to make up," Mel protested.

"I meant the metaphorical here, I didn't say I was here at my house specifically," Amelia cried. Tears were streaming down her cheeks now.

"How was I supposed to know that?" Mel shot back.

"You could have asked!" Amelia snapped.

Mel rubbed the back of her neck. "I know, I'm sorry," she said. "When I got here and you weren't here I was going to leave but Eliza said you would be home soon…"

Eliza. Goddamnit. Amelia was so upset that she'd almost forgotten what she'd known the second she'd seen them together. *This was Eliza's doing.* Amelia rubbed her temples. "I can't do this here. Not with her…" Amelia didn't know exactly what it was but suddenly being in her house was as uncomfortable as wearing an itchy sweater. She needed to get out.

"Come back to my place," Mel offered.

Amelia shook her head. "No. I…" She hesitated. Part of her wanted to run away, back to her sister's house, and never come back—never see Mel or Eliza again. But looking at Mel's beautiful face, Amelia knew she wasn't ready to give up on this yet. But that didn't mean she was ready to go home with her either. "I just need a walk."

Amelia turned and walked out the door, with Mel scrambling to follow. It wasn't raining anymore. Rainwater dripped from the trees but above the branches the sky was dark and clear.

Amelia and Mel walked in silence for a while. Amelia didn't know what to say. The thing that bothered her the most, she realized, was how unsurprised she was by Eliza's behavior. They'd been friends for so long, but Eliza had never been good with boundaries. But she never would have expected Mel to give in to Eliza's behavior. *They were talking. If she told Mel how she could help, is that why Mel let her...*

"Eliza has a whole plan on how to help you. Did she tell you?" Amelia asked.

"Yeah, she did," Mel confirmed.

"Oh."

There was one more reason why Amelia wished she hadn't ever told Eliza about Mel's problems: it had given Eliza an in. Amelia had brought Eliza into Mel's life and when Eliza came into somebody's life, she made sure things went her way.

What if Eliza really can help her? Would that be worth forgiving her for what she did tonight? Amelia weighed the hurt of what Eliza had done against the aid she still could give to Mel. She tried to reconcile the years of friendship—all the things Eliza had ever done for her—against this betrayal.

"I think you should still take her help," Amelia said. "It's the smart thing to do. I can talk to her tomorrow—"

"Fucking hell," Mel muttered. She let out a snort of laughter.

"What are you laughing about?" Amelia said, stopping to stare at Mel.

"I never thought I'd be grateful for the way Heidi ripped my life apart," Mel said. "But looking at you and Eliza, I think I am."

"What does that even mean?" Amelia asked, confused.

"Heidi used me, hurt me, and tore my world upside down. But at least she did it blatantly and quickly. In the end, anyway." Mel took a deep breath. "I wasted months of my life on her but now I'm free and I've learned so much from the experience. Eliza has been punching holes in your life for *years*. She manipulates you; she sabotages your relationships; she tears you down every day. But she always keeps the damage *just* light enough; she makes herself *just* helpful enough that you're convinced that, on balance, she's good for you, so you don't leave. But she's *not*. You give her credit for pushing you to talk to me, but we were already talking. Without her it may have taken us longer to get together but without her our first date might have actually been fun. She encouraged you not to trust me—to follow me—when I'd told you I had dark things in my life I wasn't ready to share."

"But if we hadn't been there when Brad beat you up—" Amelia began to protest.

"She didn't even want you to get out of the fucking car to help me!" Mel said.

Amelia looked down. It was true. *So why am I defending her?*

"What happened tonight…" Mel sighed. She pulled out her hair-tie and ran her fingers through her hair. "The more I think about what happened… the wine, the way she started things… She *assaulted* me, Amelia."

It was hard to hear, but Amelia knew Mel was right. Even without seeing the whole thing, she knew Mel was right.

"If you can't see that makes her a bad person, I don't know what to do."

"I…" Amelia didn't know what to say. She felt a deep sense of guilt. Eliza was her friend and because of that she felt responsible for what Eliza had done tonight.

Mel took Amelia's hand in hers. "I love you," she said.

"I love you too," Amelia whispered back.

"I don't want to lose you," Mel continued, and Amelia felt her heart squeeze painfully in her chest. Mel continued, "But I can't do this with her in the picture."

"I don't want her in the picture," Amelia whispered.

"What?"

"I don't want her in the picture," Amelia repeated at a more normal volume. "She's toxic and mean and all the things you said. I know."

"Why do I get the feeling that there's a 'but' coming?" Mel asked, tilting her head and looking intently at Amelia with her beautiful brown eyes so filled with emotion.

"But it's not that easy," Amelia said. "She's family. I know I need to get away from her but knowing the truth of that… sucks. And hurts. I spent so many years with her. We had good times too, you know."

"Of course you did. If it was all bad you never would have stayed with her this long. Amelia, you're in an abusive relationship. She might not be your partner, but it's still a relationship."

Those words were a shock to hear, but Amelia couldn't honestly disagree. She nodded.

Mel squeezed her hand. "I want to be with you, and to save you from this abuse the same way you wanted to save me. But you have to want me to help."

Amelia smiled faintly. "If you let me help you, I'll let you help me," she said.

Mel smiled back. "It's a deal."

Amelia leaned forward and kissed Mel. Mel's hand came to rest on her cheek, pulling her deeper into the kiss. The sense of relief Amelia found in Mel's kisses was overwhelming. Her life felt whole again when her lips were pressed against Mel's.

When their lips parted Amelia looked around, truly aware of her surroundings for the first time since they'd left the house. They were standing at the street corner, just outside North River. Amelia had walked there without even thinking about it. Now that she was aware of her surroundings, Amelia also suddenly realized how cold it was outside. She shivered.

Mel noticed and rubbed her shoulders. "Do you want to go inside?" she asked.

"Is that okay? It looks closed," Amelia replied.

Mel looked at her watch and then up at the window where the neon 'open' sign sat dark. "I guess Sebastian closed early," she said. "But that's okay, I have a key. Let's go inside before you freeze to death."

Amelia agreed and Mel led them in through the back door. She disabled the alarm and flicked on the light above the bar. "Here, let me get you something to help you warm up," Mel said, digging through bottles of liquor.

As Mel fixed her a drink, Amelia looked out at the dining room. It was so quiet, every clank of the bottles seemed to echo through the empty restaurant. It was odd, but somehow North River felt more like a home than a bar in that moment. The quiet was cozy, not oppressive.

"Here you go," Mel said, sliding a cocktail to Amelia. "It's one of my own concoctions—guaranteed to put a little fire in your belly."

Amelia sipped it cautiously. It was good but strong, with a hint of cinnamon and sweetness. Amelia took another sip before setting it down.

"It's good," she said. "But I think I know a better way to warm up."

Amelia pulled Mel close and kissed her. Warmth spread through her chest and out to her fingertips as they kissed. Mel lifted Amelia onto the bar; Amelia pulled off Mel's shirt. They kissed.

"Is this okay?" Amelia asked. "Doing this here?"

"Are you kidding? Having sex on the bar is basically a rite of passage," Mel replied as she ran her hands under Amelia's skirt, pulling at her panties. Amelia lifted her hips to let Mel slide them off.

"Then get up here with me," Amelia demanded as she crossed her arms and pulled her shirt up and over her head. Mel didn't hesitate.

The smooth wood of the bar was cold against the bare skin of Amelia's back, but Mel's body pressed on top of her was warm. Mel relieved Amelia of her bra, and Amelia did the same for Mel. When Amelia's hands went to the waist of Mel's pants, she stopped.

"Wait, where did you get these clothes?" she asked.

Mel winced. "Eliza gave them to me. I walked to your house in the rain and she insisted." Mel's tone was defensive and unsure.

"It's okay," Amelia said. She grinned wickedly. "Let's just get you out of them."

They made love on the bar with the desperate passion of two people who knew they'd almost lost each other and never wanted that to happen again.

When they were done, Mel brought a blanket and pillow out from the back and the two curled up in Amelia's booth and fell happily asleep.

Chapter 19: Mel

When the dust from her last interaction with Eliza had settled, Mel promised Amelia that she would ask for help. And she did—just not from Eliza. Mel set her ego aside and told Pat and Nancy the full truth of her situation. They couldn't have been more supportive—as was the rest of the North River crew. The next time Brad showed up, Carlos and the other kitchen staff were ready for him. Every blow he'd ever dealt to Mel was paid back with interest. He slunk away knowing full well that, should he show in Mel's life again, he'd be *lucky* if the cops got to him first.

Although Mel didn't get help from Eliza directly, the confidence Eliza had displayed in her ability to deal with the landlord gave Mel enough confidence of her own to seek professional assistance. Mel was able to find a lawyer who could do all the things Eliza had promised. It took months, and by the end of it, Mel was still broke as hell, but the nightmare was finally over.

It hadn't been easy for Amelia to move out of the house she'd shared with Eliza for so long, but despite all the guilt and insult Eliza threw at her, Amelia had stuck to her guns.

When Amelia moved in with Mel, the little loft transformed from stark and functional to warm and inviting. It felt like home. It wouldn't be their forever home, but it was perfect for now.

"Hey, pretty lady, how are you doing?" Mel asked as Amelia sat down in her usual seat at the bar.

"I'm great, actually. Did you know that today is the one-year anniversary of when I first met you?" Amelia asked.

Mel grinned. "You don't say."

Amelia nodded. "I figured we'd probably celebrate our real anniversary soon but… Here." She slid a card across the bar. Mel opened it. Inside, in Amelia's perfect handwriting, was a sonnet.

> *So are you to my thoughts as food to life,*
> *Or as sweet-season'd showers are to the ground;*
> *And for the peace of you I hold such strife*
> *As 'twixt a miser and his wealth is found;*
> *Now proud as an enjoyer and anon*

Doubting the filching age will steal his treasure,
Now counting best to be with you alone,
Then better'd that the world may see my
pleasure;
Sometime all full with feasting on your sight
And by and by clean starved for a look;
Possessing or pursuing no delight,
Save what is had or must from you be took.
Thus do I pine and surfeit day by day,
Or gluttoning on all, or all away.

William Shakespeare, Sonnet LXXV

"Do you like it?" Amelia asked, when Mel had set down the card.

"I liked your sonnet better," Mel replied with a wink. "But yes, I do. And I have something for you." Mel turned and walked back to the kitchen, returning with her latest attempt to present Amelia with a dish she would love. She set it in front of her girlfriend.

"A beet salad?" Amelia asked. "Since when is there a beet salad on the menu here?"

"If you like it, since today," Mel said as Amelia began to stab at the salad with her fork. "Make sure you get a little of everything," she said. The salad was composed of beets, arugula, chevre, sesame seeds, and a light but flavorful dressing of Mel's own design.

Amelia looked a little nervous as she took her first bite—probably because Mel was staring at her so intently—but once the food was in her mouth, her eyes went wide.

"Oh wow," she said through a mouthful of food. "That's *good*."

Mel watched with growing delight as Amelia shoveled the salad into her mouth. She'd never seen Amelia eat something with so much enthusiasm. It was incredibly satisfying to see. She'd made something that Amelia was genuinely happy to eat. The victory was twice as sweet because Pat and Nancy had already approved it.

"I'm glad you like it, because it's going on the new menu," Mel said, handing Amelia a mock-up print of North River's newly updated menu.

"*My Salad Beets for Amelia*?" Amelia read. "What if I'd hated it?"

"I like to think I know you well enough to know you wouldn't *hate* it, gorgeous," Mel said with her signature lop-sided grin.

Amelia shook her head, smiling. "I suppose you do. But since you designed it, shouldn't it have your name in it?" she asked.

"Nah, I already got my name in there once, no need to be greedy."

"You did?" Amelia's eyes scanned the menu until she spotted it. "Mel's Mouthwatering Roast Turkey Club? They let you put *two* things on the menu?"

"Three actually, but the third one is just called the Fancy Pants Grilled Cheese. It's rich and delicious and you'd absolutely hate it." Mel pointed to the menu. "But I did mention to Carlos and Nancy that there weren't a lot of light options, and they added and tweaked a few other things that I think you might like."

"You're amazing," Amelia said, smiling her bright dimpled smile that made Mel's heart melt.

"I've got the best inspiration," Mel replied. "Speaking of inspiration, what are you working on today? Some Chad's paper on manifest destiny?"

Amelia snickered and shook her head. "Nope. I'm taking today for myself and making it a book day."

"That's great!" Mel was so proud of Amelia. Once they'd moved in together Mel had encouraged Amelia to take advantage of the cheaper cost of living and cut down on her clients to give herself time to write for herself. Amelia had been hesitant and unsure of herself at first, but eventually she'd found her groove and now Mel looked forward to every 'book day.' Amelia was just so *happy* on book days. And often a little extra horny. There was just something about tapping into her passion for writing that awakened Amelia's passion for everything else.

"So, are you ever going to tell me what the book's about?" Mel asked as she took away Amelia's empty plate to make room for her to pull out her laptop.

"Nope," Amelia replied. "You're just going to have to wait to read it."

"Well, then I'd better leave you alone to write, pretty writer lady." She winked. Mel began to walk away but Amelia reached across the bar and grabbed her hand.

"Wait," she said. "Mel?"

"Yes?"

"Thank you."

"For what?" Mel asked.

"For this year. For you. For everything. I thought my life was pretty okay when I walked in here for the first time, but now… it's amazing. And I have you to thank for that." Amelia squeezed her hand. Mel squeezed it back.

"I love you, Amelia. No words can do justice to what you've meant to me this past year, so I'm not going to even try. I'm just glad you braved—what did you call it? Blood River Mob Front?"

Amelia laughed. "Yeah. Me too."